NECESSARY PROOF

A CHRISTIAN ROMANTIC SUSPENSE NOVELLA

SONOMA SERIES
BOOK 4.1

CAMY TANG

Camy's Books

Sushi series

Sushi for One?

"The Sushi Toss" (short story)

Only Uni

Single Sashimi

Weddings and Wasabi (novella)

"White Soup" (short story)

The Lone Rice Ball

Protection for Hire Series

Protection for Hire

A Dangerous Stage

Sonoma Series

Deadly Intent

Formula for Danger

Stalker in the Shadows

Narrow Escape

Necessary Proof (novella)

Unshakeable Pursuit

Treacherous Intent

Gone Missing

Mahina Security series

Bento and Betrayal (novella)

The Lone Rice Ball

Sushi and Suspicions

Year of the Dog

Warubozu Spa Chronicles

The Wedding Kimono (novella)

Devotional

Who I Want to Be

1

For the second time in his life, Alex Villa was accused of a crime. Except that this time, he didn't do it.

He crept through the underbrush, trying not to crunch the dry grass under his work boots, with his eyes on the figure of the lean man in a dirty T-shirt and torn jeans who strode confidently through the trees thirty yards ahead.

It was difficult to stay hidden from the man because the trees here on Harman Ridge in Sonoma County were scraggly, and even the hardy oaks and laurels looked a little shriveled after the dry winter. Soon, the spring rains would turn the California foothills green again, but today the sun beat hot, and the dry undergrowth threatened to give away Alex's presence to the man he was following.

At first glance, the man had looked like a Hispanic migrant worker, with darkly tanned skin and straight midnight hair. But every so often, his shirt would hike up and reveal tattoos across his lower back of strange writing. The letters weren't the standard English alphabet, and certainly not Spanish. The swirling symbols twisted with the movement of the man's torso as he clambered over manzanita and slithered between juniper bushes.

This man had started the stories about the meth lab near Graves Peak, the stories that had begun Alex's recent troubles. This man was the one who had framed him. This man was the reason Alex was facing prison. Again.

He had to pause to take a deep, sharp breath. Prison had been a brutal place, and the memories were like dark ghosts that hovered at the edges of his vision. But prison had also been a place where his life had taken a drastic turn and he'd found peace for the first time in years. He'd found love. He'd found Christ.

The memory calmed the churning in his stomach, and he hunched lower and crept after the man. He'd been feeling mildly nauseated since Detective Carter had reluctantly revealed the "evidence" against Alex. He'd been released, but he wasn't about to wait around to see what other planted evidence would surface that would enable the Sonoma police to convict him.

The trees grew thicker here, and he hung back even more. If this was a second meth lab site, there would be more people around guarding it.

But there weren't other guards. The man headed directly for a mobile home that seemed sunken deep into the scrub brush. A narrow, deeply rutted trail ran from the building back down the other side of the ridge, where the distance to the nearest road was several miles. In contrast, he and the man had been walking cross country from the opposite direction for only about twenty minutes.

With no guards and only a few people aware of this remote location, this lab site would be difficult for law enforcement to find.

Not anymore. He would inform Detective Carter about this meth lab, too, just as soon as …

He clenched his jaw. Just as soon as he cleared his name. He'd forgotten about his predicament for a pitiful moment. He was no longer a trusted confidential informant for the Sonoma PD. Instead, he was implicated in a police officer's murder.

He circled the mobile home. An acrid toxic gas burned his nostrils, and he gagged at a combination of cat urine and rotten egg smells that wafted over him, emanating from the chemicals in the lab. The drone of a generator almost drowned out the sound of voices, and he crept toward the other side of the trailer. He lay on his stomach and peered through the weeds.

The man he had followed was talking rapidly to two other men. After a few minutes, Alex recognized the language as Filipino. He'd known several Filipino gang members in prison, and after he came to Christ, he was still friends with some of them, visiting the two still in prison and doing what he could to help the others stay out of jail. Two of them had come to church with Alex once.

He had suspected the language of the man's tattoos were Filipino. It looked like a Filipino gang was involved. Not a big surprise. Alex was friends with many of the local farm workers, who had mentioned seeing more and more Filipino strangers in the area in the past couple years. It matched what Detective Carter had told him about the Tumibay Filipino gang, based in San Francisco, who had been ramping up meth production in the rural areas outside of Sonoma.

The two men he talked to were a study of opposites. One was taller, dressed in a dirty, long-sleeved shirt and jeans despite the heat, sweat running down his shaved head. He was lean, and some wicked knife wound scars running across his left cheek made him look as if he had a permanent one-sided sneer.

The other man was shorter and even more slender, but with paler skin and long black hair pulled into a ponytail. His polo shirt and shorts, while casual, were expensive, as was his watch. He wore glasses, although they couldn't have been very strong because they barely distorted his heavy-lidded black eyes.

Both men responded in Filipino, and the shorter one gestured to a nearby folding table and chair set up several feet away from the mobile home, near the generator that powered the meth lab. A laptop stood open on the table.

The men argued for a few minutes more, then the one he had followed turned and stomped away, back the way he'd come. Alex flattened himself further into the grass, glad he hadn't remained behind the man. He'd have been spotted in a heartbeat.

The two men stood and talked in low voices. From their body language, they appeared to be equals in authority, despite the differences in dress. Another man's voice called from inside the trailer, and the taller one went back into the lab.

The shorter man pulled out a cell phone and frowned at it. He then lifted it up, still staring, and walked in a widening circle.

Straight toward Alex.

God, don't let him find me. He stilled, hearing his heartbeat in his ears. His dark shirt and khaki pants made him hard to spot against the undergrowth, but it wouldn't matter if the man simply stumbled over him.

The man stopped, then backtracked, still staring at his phone. He moved around the trailer and away from Alex while dialing someone. His voice carried over the sound of the generator as he seemed to be giving instructions to someone in rapid Filipino.

Alex made his decision in the space of time between one breath and another.

He leaped to his feet and sprinted to the table. He closed the laptop as quietly as he could and unplugged the power cord, which tangled among some other electrical equipment under the table which he hadn't noticed. One looked like an external hard drive, snarled in a mass of wires. He reached for it, but the man's voice grew louder again.

No time to unplug the external hard drive. Alex took the laptop and ran. He didn't bother to hide the noise as he crashed through bushes and circled around the other side of the trailer. He picked up speed as he headed back the direction he'd come, jumping over bushes and dodging trees.

Shouts sounded behind him, but he didn't look back. There was the crack of a gunshot, and he ducked his head but tried not to slow his speed. More gunshots, but he heard the bullets hit trees several yards behind him. They stopped firing, probably since the trees made him a more difficult target to hit.

He sprinted past the tattooed man that he had followed. The man was several yards away, but apparently unarmed. All he could do was shout as Alex dashed by.

On the way to the meth lab, they'd taken a straight route through the wilderness, about a mile or a little more. The man had parked on the remote access road at the back of old Mr. Rivers's farm, but Alex, trying not to be seen tailing him, had parked on an unused farm track on Mr. Rivers's property, hidden from the road by rows of dead grape vines.

Once out of the trees, he raced for his truck. He stumbled over some clods of dirt from the unused track and nearly dropped the laptop, but he was used to keeping his balance in uneven dirt thanks to his hours working in the fields of his mama's farm and in his brother's greenhouses, and he was able to right himself quickly. He scrounged in his pocket for his car keys and hit the unlock button only a second before he yanked the door open.

As he turned over the engine, the three men he'd seen exploded from the tree line and dashed toward him. The tallest man was in front, and he now pulled out his gun and fired again. Alex ducked low as his window exploded in a cloudy spiderweb of cracks around the bullet hole. He slammed his foot on the accelerator and the truck leaped forward.

More shots, but these hit the frame of his truck. He bumped and jolted down the farm track, but quickly skidded to turn onto the access road. He looked in his rearview mirror and saw the men running toward the tattooed man's car, but he was far down the road before they even reached it. He slid onto the curvy highway that wound through the foothills, and after a few turns, pulled into the long driveway belonging to the farm of a family he knew. He parked behind a stand of trees a little ways back from the road and waited.

The tattooed man's car soon passed by the driveway.

Alex leaned back against the seat. He'd wait to make sure they didn't double back, then he'd find his way to the main highway to Sonoma.

He laid his hand on the laptop on the passenger seat. He was comfortable with electronics, but he was a hardware guy. He understood enough software to know he was a bull in a china shop, so he didn't want to fiddle with the computer in case it had a security feature.

He needed help. He needed to clear his name. His race for his life couldn't have been for nothing.

Jane Lawton nearly dropped her steaming pot of Mac-N-Cheese at the sound of a powerful fist knocking at her apartment door. "Coming!" She spooned the gooey, bad-for-you goodness into a bowl, then ran some water in the pot in the sink.

The urgent knocking sounded again. Somehow it didn't sound like one of her neighbors, wanting Jane's help with a computer problem. She looked through the peephole.

She felt a sharp pulse at the base of her throat. "Alex?" She opened the door.

Normally a walking Calvin Klein ad, he now had a grim, serious cast to his face as he hurriedly entered her apartment with a messenger bag slung across one broad shoulder. "Quick, close the door."

"What's going on?" She locked the deadbolt.

It frightened her that he looked so different now, lacking his usual smile and dimples. "I need your help, Jane."

She couldn't control the bitterness that burned the back of her throat. It seemed that was the only thing she was good for, helping the men in her life so they could leave her and move on. She swallowed and said carefully, "Doing what?"

He pulled a laptop from his messenger bag. "There's information on this that I need, but I'm not sure if there's any type of security protecting it."

"Whoa." Jane took a step back. "You're saying that's not your laptop, and you want me to get into it? What's going on?" She knew he had been in prison for a few years, but she thought he'd put his illegal past behind him.

He scrubbed his hand over his high forehead. "It's not what it looks like."

"That makes it sound even worse."

He exhaled and seemed to study her. His intent, dark eyes made her squirm. She knew she'd changed a lot in the past year. She'd only spoken to him once in all that time, a few months ago at the party celebrating his brother's engagement to Rachel, Jane's second cousin but as close as a sister. After a minute or two of chit-chat, he had been quick to leave her to speak to Detective Carter, which had given her a pang even though she hadn't been in a sociable mood. What a difference from when she and Alex had first met years ago. He had seemed interested in her, but she'd been ...

She shoved the memories aside. "I'm only going to ask this one more time. What's going on?"

"I just ... I can trust you, right?"

"Trust me with what?"

"Could I sit down? Have some coffee?" He sniffed. "Is that Mac-N-Cheese?"

"Did you want some?"

He gave her a smile that caused that sharp pulse at the base of her throat again. "I haven't eaten since breakfast."

And it was already past seven. "But it's Mac-N-Cheese. From a box."

"So?"

"You eat Mac-N-Cheese? Isn't your mother good enough to be on Iron Chef or something like that?"

The smile disappeared, and long lines were drawn on either side of his mouth. "I haven't been home all day."

The wooden tone of his voice made Jane wonder if he hadn't gone home because he couldn't, not because he chose not to. Unlike Jane, Alex and his brother had a solid relationship with their mother and would do anything to protect her.

The combination living room/dining room in her one-bedroom apartment was currently her office, so she hastily swept aside some electrical equipment and notes from the dining table and set them in a neat stack on the floor. "Have a seat. I don't have decaf coffee."

He sank into a wooden chair with a sigh. "I need leaded right now, anyway."

As she retrieved her bowl of food from the kitchen, she eyed his six-foot-plus frame, at least two hundred pounds of solid muscle. She set the entire thing in front of him. "Go ahead."

"No—" he began.

"I'll cook some eggs."

His eyes softened. "Thanks, Jane."

She tried not to think of those eyes as she started the coffee maker and whisked eggs with soy sauce. He made her feel … special, and she couldn't trust her own feelings anymore. Rachel had accused her of becoming too cynical this past year, but could anyone blame her after what had happened?

So in her frying pan, she scrambled the eggs mixed with soy sauce and served it on some rice she'd heated in the microwave. "Shoyu-egg-rice," as her Japanese mother called it, and it was Jane's comfort food. She needed comfort right now, in preparing to deal with the handsome man at her dining table and whatever trouble he'd brought into her home.

When she returned to the dining table, he had just finished the Mac-N-Cheese, but she had anticipated that. She served him some of the eggs and rice. "Here."

He frowned at the brown-colored scrambled eggs. "What's this?"

"Japanese-style breakfast. Try it."

She bowed her head to say grace, but she felt self-conscious. Not because he wasn't Christian, because she knew he was, but she only said grace these days out of habit. She'd been feeling like a chasm had opened between her and God. She couldn't understand why He'd allowed her to be so hurt, and maybe her distrust of men had extended to Him, too.

She took a bite of salty egg, hot rice, and remembered breakfasts at home with her mom and her brother, a peaceful and innocent time before she'd been aware of how little her father had cared for her.

Of how little anyone cared for her, apparently.

"This is good." He paused from shoveling food into his mouth. "What's wrong?"

She realized she'd been frowning into her bowl. "Nothing." She stabbed at the rice with her fork. "That should be my question."

He grimaced and slowed his eating. "Look, Jane …"

"I want the full version. Not the version you'd tell your mama."

The glance he sent her could almost have been playful, but Jane steeled herself against the dimples that appeared briefly in his cheeks. "It's a little unnerving how you can read me, Jane."

"You're stalling." She could hear the coffeemaker burbling. "You don't get coffee until you explain yourself."

He took the last bite of eggs and rice and pushed the bowl away from him. "I'm being set up, Jane, and I have to clear my name. You heard about the police officer who died in that shoot-out at a meth lab in the foothills last week?"

She nodded.

His face tightened and he stared at her wooden tabletop. "That man is dead because of me."

2

After a beat of shock, Jane said, "Aren't you being a little melodramatic? The paper said it was a gang member who shot him."

"I gave the police the location of that meth lab, but it was a trap."

"How did you know about the lab?"

He ran a tanned hand through his short, dark hair. "I know a lot of the farm workers around Sonoma, and some of them found out about the lab and told me."

"How'd they find it?"

"A meth lab smells pretty potent."

"Oh."

"I told Detective Carter, but there were gang members waiting for the Sonoma PD to arrive."

She could see how he might feel it was his fault. "There's no way you could have known that would happen."

"Then the next day, five thousand dollars were deposited into my bank account from an offshore account."

"From who?"

He shook his head. "I don't know. I told Detective Carter about the deposit right away, but it looks like I was paid to tell the Sonoma PD about the lab so they'd get gunned down. I'm under investigation."

"But you help Detective Carter all the time. Doesn't that count for something?" When Jane had first met Alex, she'd overheard the detective asking to speak to him about helping the police with a case. Alex's brother, Edward, had explained to her that Alex was a confidential informant for the Sonoma PD. Alex was friends with many of the farm workers in Sonoma, and if they had a concern, they told him, who would tell the detective. This roundabout way to get information to the police protected the identities of people who weren't comfortable going to the police directly.

"Detective Carter knows I'm innocent, but it looks bad." A muscle in his jaw flexed. "I'm being set up. I'm thinking that it's only a matter of time before the police find planted evidence that will get me convicted."

He must feel trapped. Suffocating. It would be intolerable to someone like him, who was full of life, full of energy, and always transparent. "I'm sorry." She touched his forearm.

She didn't feel a jolt, but something about touching him made her feel … different. As if he'd flipped on some switch inside her.

She snatched her hand back and stood up. "I'll get the coffee."

She had to remember this was Alex, for goodness' sake. She'd known him for a few years already. What was more, when they'd first met, he'd asked her out to dinner, and she'd turned him down, admitting that she was interested in someone else.

And she had been, at the time. She'd had grand hopes of a lasting, meaningful relationship built on respect.

What a colossal idiot she'd been to think there was anything about herself that would attract anyone.

But Alex had been attracted to you, a small voice whispered.

Except she was no longer that woman he'd asked out on a date. And she never would be again.

She needed to focus on the issue right now. She put his coffee in front of him, black, the way he liked it. "Who's setting you up? Although if people know you help the police, that list might be long."

"I know exactly who it is. The Tumibays."

The Filipino gang who had meth labs scattered in the wilderness areas around Sonoma. "The police raided a few of their labs in the past few months. You told the police about them?"

He nodded. "I found out from some day laborers. Lots of people are worried about the meth. Kids are getting addicted, especially in the poorer areas."

"I know," Jane said in a low voice. "Monica was telling me that there have been more and more meth overdose cases at her free children's clinic."

"I've been following up on any leads I can ferret out about the Tumibays. They threatened me a few times." He shrugged. "They soon figured out it wouldn't work. But then they tried to attack Mama."

"When did this happen?" Jane sat up in her chair. "Is she all right?"

"She's fine. It was a month ago. I was at the greenhouses, but three of the farmhands live with us at the house, and they held the gang off until the police arrived. They arrested the gang captain in charge of the meth operation here in Sonoma."

"So shouldn't that have ended it all?"

"There's a new captain the Tumibays sent to take over the operation."

Jane finally saw what was happening. "The new captain is trying to ruin your reputation with the police. He saw that threatening you or your family wasn't effective."

"After the officer was killed, I went to talk to the farm workers who told me about the meth lab in the first place. They had heard about it from a day laborer who spoke Spanish with a strange accent. I have a couple Filipino friends who speak Spanish with an accent, and I thought he might have been planted by the Tumibays. I found the guy and followed him to Graves Peak." He told her about the meth lab and the three men he'd seen.

"So you stole the laptop from the new Tumibay captain?"

"No, it wasn't the captain. I know what Talaba looks like. These were just his men."

"Still." Jane stared at the innocuous-looking laptop. "You should turn this in to the police."

"And tell them I found another meth lab? How convenient. If they were on the fence about if I'm involved with the Tumibays, I'm sure that wouldn't change their minds *at all*."

"But they're the *police*—"

"And they think I gave them information that got one of their own killed. I'm not their favorite person at this moment. If I hand this laptop to them, they're going to view it with suspicion. They're not going to be careful about any kind of data it might have, because I could be feeding them more false leads. If it were my laptop, I'd set up security protocols in case it was taken, some program to erase sensitive data. That means we only get one shot at this, and the data on this computer might be the only thing to clear my name." He reached out to cover her hand with his. "Jane, you're the only one I know who can find a way to bypass any security protocols."

His palm was large and warm. Derek used to touch her like this, and it had made her stomach flutter like it did right now with Alex.

She pulled her hand away from him.

Could she trust him? She'd trusted Derek and look how that had gone.

But she knew Alex. She trusted his brother, Edward. And the fact he was being set up, that people who knew him were no longer believing him, must feel like a spear to the gut. She knew, because it had felt that way when her father hadn't believed her.

She wanted to help him because she couldn't let someone else feel he was being abandoned by his friends.

At that moment, her neighbor's dog began barking. "That's strange," Jane murmured before she could stop herself.

"What's strange?" He had grown tense.

She shook her head. "I'm being paranoid after what you've been talking about."

He gave her a hard look. "Just tell me, Jane."

"Well, Wiley—the dog—hardly ever barks. Sarah's a dog trainer, and her well-behaved pets are a point of professional pride for her."

His eyes narrowed. "Now that I think about it, the dog didn't bark when I came to your apartment."

"The last time Wiley barked was when some kids were fooling around on the fire escape."

There was a heartbeat of silence, then he shot to his feet. "Jane, get down."

To her credit, Jane didn't ask why or demand to know what was happening. She stared at him with her wide, gold-flecked brown eyes for a moment, then she dropped to her knees.

"Where's the fire escape?" he asked.

"Bedroom window."

He snapped off the lights as he made his way to the dark bedroom. The dog's yapping pierced through several apartment walls to reach his ears, but he hoped it masked the sound as he eased open the sliding glass window. He grabbed a small facial mirror propped up on Jane's dressing table and stuck a corner out the window. It took him a bit of tilting to find the right angle to see the fire escape balcony.

There was a man on the fire escape, heading his way.

He had to get Jane out of here. He'd guess there was also a man heading down the hallway toward Jane's apartment. It's what he would do, in this situation.

Thank You, Father God. If the dog hadn't barked, or Jane hadn't noticed, they might have been trapped. He'd figure out later how they'd found him.

He weighed his options. The fire escape was narrow and difficult fighting terrain, but he didn't know how many men were nearing the front door, whereas there was only one outside Jane's window.

He hurried to the bedroom door and gestured to Jane. "Grab the laptop," he said in a quiet voice.

She scurried toward him, shoving the laptop into the messenger bag he'd brought with him.

"Stay down," he told her, "but be ready to follow me."

She nodded. Her face was even paler in the dimness of her bedroom, and he saw the trembling in her hands, but she had a firm determination to her chin.

He hesitated beside the open window. He had only one shot at this. He took a deep breath, then lightly leaped over the sill onto the fire escape.

His boots hit the metal with a clang. He immediately sprinted toward the man, who was only a few feet away now.

The man had stiffened when Alex appeared out of the window, and he hadn't yet recovered when Alex barreled into him. The man was shorter but still taller than average, and even though Alex had had the element of surprise when he attacked, the man was faster. His elbow snapped out, and although Alex ducked his head, the blow grazed his temple.

The two of them hit the floor of the balcony with a thundering shudder from the metal. The narrow width of the fire escape and Alex's broad shoulders made his punches awkward, and his blows were weaker than his sparring sessions at the gym with his buddies. But he only needed to incapacitate the man until he and Jane could get away.

Alex grabbed a fistful of shirt and slammed the frontal bone of his own skull into the man's face. He felt rather than heard the man's nose break, and blood spurted across his cheek. The man gave a sharp groan of pain, and Alex followed with a jab to the jaw.

The man's body stiffened, then fell back. He wasn't completely out because his arms waved feebly, but Alex yelled, "Jane!"

She was already climbing out the window with the messenger bag thrown over her shoulder. Her eyes slid over the man as she leaped over his body on the fire escape, but she didn't glance back as she followed Alex down the stairs.

They were on the ground in seconds since Jane was only on the third floor. He had his truck keys, but realized the men probably knew the make and model of his pickup. "Do you have your car keys?"

Jane pulled the keys from her slacks pocket. "Over here." Luckily, her parking slot was near the fire escape.

Of course, her car was practical and sensible, like her. The hybrid would be uncomfortable for him to sit in, much less drive. He shook his head when she offered him the keys.

She stared for a quick moment. "Really? Not what I would have expected from a guy." She scrambled into the driver's seat.

"I'm secure in my masculinity," he couldn't resist teasing. As they buckled up, he added, "Besides, I'm probably better than you at spotting a tail."

She backed out of the parking slot like a rocket, slamming his body against the seatbelt. He thought her driving might be attributed to nerves, until she got onto the street.

The woman drove like a maniac. Who knew that lurking under Jane's neutral colored, professional clothing was a *Grand Theft Auto* leaderboard winner?

"Where to?" The tires screeched a little as she took a corner onto the expressway.

"Into traffic." He searched the cars behind them. "If we're being followed, it won't hurt to be somewhere we can try to lose them."

She wove between cars, darting left and right without warning and without hitting the brakes. He had to grab the door handle so he wouldn't fly out of his seat.

"See anyone?" She finally had to brake hard when she cut in front of a minivan and behind a convertible who had just moved into the lane.

"I think we're safe," he said.

She eased up on the gas a minuscule amount. "Now where to?"

He nodded toward the backseat, where she'd tossed the messenger bag containing the laptop. "Anywhere you can get the information off of that computer."

"You're kidding, right?"

"What do you mean?"

Jane turned exasperated eyes to his. "All the equipment I needed to examine that laptop is in a place currently crawling with Filipino gang members—my apartment."

3

Even though it looked like they'd lost anyone trying to follow them, Alex closely observed the cars around them as he directed Jane outside of Sonoma toward Jorge's tavern. It was in a remote area, he had a lot of friends there, and more importantly, he'd left his computer toolbox there last week.

Jane turned into the tiny dirt parking lot in front of the brown building. It stood in a small lot between two orchards, both in bud with new fruits soon to appear as spring swept into the county. His expert gardening nose smelled cherry blossoms as he unfolded himself from Jane's car and stretched.

"Does Jorge have wireless internet?" Jane grabbed the laptop from the backseat.

"No, he's hard-wired."

"How close is the nearest house?"

"A couple miles in either direction." He nodded toward the narrow road that fronted the tavern. "There's only farms and orchards in this area. Why?"

"I'm probably being overly cautious, but I don't know what kind of security this computer has. The security program might be instructed to find the nearest wireless network and broadcast data so the owner can find it again."

"And you don't want there to be a wireless network it can find."

"Exactly. And you said you don't know anything about software." Jane's tone was almost teasing, although her eyes were still somber from the events of only an hour ago.

"I know only enough to make me dangerous." He led the way up to the narrow front porch, then opened one of the two swinging double doors to the tavern.

It had been an old farmhouse before Jorge bought it for his tavern, useless because the farmland had been sold around it. He'd torn down most of the walls on the first floor in order to put in scarred, mismatched tables and chairs, but there was still the stairs to the second floor living quarters on one side of the front hallway. There was no one inside except the deeply tanned, old Hispanic man standing behind the counter at the back of the front room, near the kitchen door.

"Alejandro!" Jorge raised his hands in greeting and waved them toward the counter.

In Spanish, Alex said, "Thanks for letting us come so late, Jorge."

"For you, anything, my friend."

Alex turned to Jane and said in English, "This is Jorge."

Jane shook Jorge's hand and surprised them both by answering in Spanish. "I'm Jane Lawton. Nice to meet you."

"You speak Spanish?" Alex asked her.

"I took it in high school." She shrugged. "And a couple of my neighbors are Hispanic, so I use it often enough."

"Are you hungry? Adelita should be almost done cooking." Jorge disappeared behind the kitchen door.

"Where's your toolbox?" Jane asked.

"Later. Adelita and Jorge rarely cook this late. They're doing it just for us."

Jane looked around the empty tavern. "Why aren't they open for dinner?"

"Jorge and Adelita started their business by making burritos and selling them cheaply to the farm hands in the fields. They got so popular that they opened this tavern, but it's for breakfast and lunch only because they still send the lunch wagon out to the fields every day. They're usually in bed by now because they get up so early."

Jane's delicate cheeks colored a strawberry pink that reminded him of some of the rare roses his brother cultivated for clients at the greenhouses. "They shouldn't have cooked for us."

"They enjoy being hospitable."

A silence fell between them that was more awkward than the silence in the car. Then, Jane had been concentrating on driving and he had been keeping an eye out for anyone following them. Here, in the quiet of the tavern, he became aware again of how beautiful she was, with her slightly slanted eyes and high cheekbones, the graceful neck just barely covered by her short, straight hair. It had been perfectly smooth when he'd arrived at her apartment, but now it looked windblown, probably from their mad dash down the fire escape.

Every time he saw her was like a kick in his gut, no matter how many times they happened to meet. He had been eager to ask her out when they first met, but she'd shyly confessed she was interested in someone else. He had been jealous of the guy who could put the glow in her cheeks and the golden glitter in her brown eyes.

But when he'd seen her at his brother's engagement party, he'd been surprised at the faint lines alongside her pink mouth, the deadness in her eyes. Someone had hurt her, badly. He'd wanted to ask, but hesitated because it was obvious she was still in pain. And in the end, Detective Carter had waved urgently to him, and he'd had to leave her to speak to him.

"How have you been lately?" The question seemed a bit lame, considering they'd spent the better part of the last two hours together. "The last time we met, you said you had a new job."

There was a flash of pain that tightened the skin around her eyes, and he wanted to kick himself. But she answered in a quiet voice, "It's fine. It pays the bills."

What a change from when they'd first met, and she'd talked excitedly about the startup she worked for and the voice recognition software she was helping to write. "Are you still writing voice software?"

Her jaw flexed before she answered him. "No. I'm doing IT support for an insurance company."

"Oh," he said faintly. Jane was brilliant. Why was she doing routine IT work rather than shining like a star at a tech startup?

She obviously didn't want to talk about it. "You're still helping to run your mama's farm?"

"And helping Edward with his greenhouse business."

"And being a CI for Sonoma PD. When do you sleep?" Her attempt at a joke didn't quite lighten the brittleness in her voice.

"All I do is talk to people, be friendly. It's not work." He liked feeling that he was helping the community. He could take risks others couldn't, like fighting against the Tumibays' meth production. What if he couldn't do it anymore? What would happen to him?

He didn't want to think about it. He *would* clear his name. He had to.

"Are you still dating that one guy?" He tried to sound casual, to hide the fact he wanted to know.

She stiffened, all her muscles rigid. "What guy?"

He just couldn't stop making things worse. "You, uh, told me about that guy at work …"

She turned her face away from him. "It didn't work out," she said in a wooden voice.

"I'm sorry." He wasn't. How long ago had it been? What kind of a loser didn't appreciate the jewel she was?

Thankfully, Jorge and his wife, Adelita, entered with steaming plates of food. Adelita laid the plate she carried in front of Alex, then reached across the counter to grasp his face and kiss his cheek. "So good to see you, Alejandro."

"You smell like cinnamon." He grinned at her. "Does that mean you made me *sopapillas?*"

She rolled her eyes. "You and your bottomless stomach."

"I just like your cooking."

Adelita then turned and kissed Jane, too, which made her cheeks flush with pleasure. "Call me Adelita."

"I'm Jane."

"Eat, eat." Adelita gestured to the plates of food.

"I'll pray for us," Alex said to Jane.

Before he bowed his head to say grace, he saw the bleakness that shuttered over Jane's eyes for a brief moment. She had always been a strong Christian. Had whatever gave her that brittle, fragile quality struck a blow against her faith in God, too?

He glanced at her as he finished saying grace, but her face was a polite mask. However, that slipped to reveal awe as she took her first bite of the bean burrito Jorge and Adelita had made.

"That's amazing," Jane said to Adelita. "You make your own tortillas?"

"Of course." Jorge seemed offended she would think he'd serve anything else.

Alex hid his smile as he wolfed down a burrito. The flour tortilla was soft and slightly crispy on the outside from being lightly pan-seared, while the beans were silky and flavorful with Adelita's secret spice mix.

Jorge set two bottles of Mexican orange soda in front of them. "Now, you tell me what kind of trouble you're in."

Alex hesitated.

"Alejandro, you must let me help you," Jorge said quietly.

So he told them about the shootout at the meth lab, about the money appearing in his bank account, about following the tattooed man to the second meth lab on Graves Peak.

Jorge's dark eyes narrowed, making the lines deepen on his broad forehead. "I know the man you speak of. The tattoo, the accent. His name is Rodrigo."

"You don't know his last name?"

"No. I saw him in the fields once, last week or the week before, but never again. He never came here with the regulars."

Many of the Filipinos Alex had known had Spanish names, so that didn't help him much. The man had probably been working in the fields in order to spread the information about the meth lab trap.

He told them about the laptop and the men at Jane's apartment. Adelita's chocolate colored eyes grew large, and she covered Jane's forearm with her hand. "You are all right?"

"I'm fine." Jane smiled and it transformed her, revealing a radiance that made his chest tighten.

"You stay here and rest tonight," Jorge said. "We have extra bedrooms."

"No, too many people will come for breakfast in the morning," he said.

"Leave before then," Adelita said. "No one will know you were here."

"Thank you."

"We must go to bed," Jorge said. "We wake at four to start breakfast."

"You know where the bedrooms are upstairs?" Adelita said, and Alex nodded. "There are fresh sheets in the hall closet."

She kissed his cheek again, then also kissed Jane. Her hands lingered on the girl's smooth hair. "Alejandro is a good man. He will take care of you."

Jane's neck turned scarlet, and her gaze dropped.

Adelita's words only reinforced his protective instinct toward Jane. He wouldn't let anything happen to her. He wanted to make sure no one hurt her ever again.

Jorge and Adelita said their goodnights, then headed up the stairs.

Jane and Alex picked at their food in silence for a while. Her neck was still red with embarrassment, and he didn't know what to say to smooth over the moment. He cleared his throat. "They're good people."

"They trust you, which makes me feel better about trusting you, too. I don't want to put them in danger."

The way he had put her in danger. "I'm sorry to drag you into this. I didn't think. I just knew I needed your help."

"Don't feel bad. I would never refuse to help you." She sipped her soda. "To help anyone," she added.

Ouch. But a part of him suspected that she was pushing him away as a defense mechanism, due to whatever had changed her so much in the past year.

He wanted to put his arms around her, to surround her with his strength so she wouldn't have anything to fear, but she had a quality of barbed self-sufficiency emanating from her body language that kept him in his seat.

She had always been quiet, serious, even geeky in her conversation, but she'd never before looked so ... desolate. What had happened to her? He knew she wouldn't tell him.

"How did those guys find you?" Jane asked. "You ditched your cell phone, right?"

He nodded. Jane had done the same within minutes of escaping her apartment.

"Did they follow you to my apartment?"

"I know they didn't, because I was looking out for them and I drove in circles for a while to make sure no one was behind me. They saw my truck, but the only way they could have tracked that was through traffic cameras."

Jane gave him a sidelong look. "If they have someone in Sonoma PD, they could have."

He hadn't thought of that. "They may not have been able to track your car here. There aren't many traffic cameras out near these farmlands."

"We probably shouldn't stay here, regardless. But they might spot my car when we leave the area."

"I know a way back to Sonoma through back roads." Before he had spoken to Jane, he had agonized about simply turning the laptop over to the police, but he'd been desperate and he knew the police hadn't trusted him, not after the death of that officer. Now he was glad he hadn't turned in the laptop. What might have happened to it if the Tumibays did indeed have a mole in the Sonoma police department?

He suddenly realized, "I didn't check the laptop for a GPS tracker."

"I'll check, but I doubt it. An installed GPS tracker requires a continuous connection to a cellular network or satellite, and I can't see a gang member who's doing illegal things on a laptop signing up for a GPS subscription that the FBI can trace back to them. Plus it's a major drain on the battery. Tracking software is more practical than GPS." She picked up the messenger bag and pulled out the laptop. "Where's your toolbox? I want to look under this baby's hood."

"Jorge said he'd leave it behind the counter for me." He slid off his stool and went behind the pitted wooden counter. His toolbox lay on the floor, and he hefted it up to set it before Jane.

"Why is your toolbox here?" She opened it and sifted through the small gauge screwdrivers.

"One of Jorge's kids gave him a larger memory card for his computer, so I came over to install it for him. Then I started playing soccer with Jorge's grandkids and stayed for dinner. After dinner, I left and forgot my toolbox here."

"You didn't need it at home?" She started unscrewing the back of the laptop.

"This is my computer toolbox. I have other toolboxes at home for the cars and the farming equipment." He was comfortable around computers, but Jane began unscrewing components left and right. "You're taking it apart without booting it up first?"

"I'm removing the wireless adapter and bluetooth card." She attacked something with a pair of tweezers. "I don't know what kind of security software it has, but if he was paranoid, he'd have installed a LoJack type of software in the UEFI that would connect to the internet as soon as it had a chance. It could even be programmed to delete sensitive data. I don't want this laptop to phone home and give our location away."

He winced as something snapped, but Jane wasn't unduly worried as she removed an electrical piece from the vicinity of the motherboard. "Hardware isn't my specialty, but if I can get the hard drive out, I might be able to use another computer to hack the information off of it."

He thought of her computer at her apartment. "What kind of computer?"

"I can't use just any computer." Jane stared at the hard drive in the laptop, chewing her bottom lip as she thought. "But there's one at my workplace."

"Those guys were at your apartment. They'll know by now where you work and they might be looking out for you."

"This late at night? And this soon after they raided my apartment?"

"You want to go tonight?"

She shrugged. "Part of the job is being on call for emergencies. I've had to go into work late at night lots of times."

"They still might be watching the building. They know you're with me and that we have the laptop, so they're not going to leave any stone unturned. At least, that's what I would do if I were a desperate drug gang captain."

Jane leaned forward over the countertop toward him, and there was a calculating light in her eyes. "What if we could get into the building without being seen?"

4

Jane shivered as she and Alex hiked across the manicured lawns of the Magnolia Scott Business Complex campus, but not from the cold. There were occasional lampposts along the cement walkways that cut between the shadowy buildings, but most of the campus was in darkness that had a deathly stillness to it. No night birds, no cicadas at this time of year, just a wet coldness to the air that seemed to make their footsteps echo even louder.

He had indeed known back roads back to Sonoma, although the potholes had made her teeth rattle. But they avoided traffic cameras, and luckily Jane's workplace was in a business complex that nestled next to the rolling foothills, not in the middle of a busy urban area. They'd driven as close as they could, then parked along the far edge of the campus to walk to the building where her company lay.

She shivered again in her cardigan, the only outerwear she'd been wearing when they ran from her apartment. He noticed.

"Are you cold?" He wrapped a large arm around her shoulders, his hand rubbing her shoulders.

She had never been this close to him before. She caught the green sweetness of basil, the woody tang of rosemary, and overlying it all was the sharp, earthy scent of his musk. It made the tension across her shoulders release, while at the same time a fluttering started in her ribcage.

She could almost pretend that she was protected, that she was cherished by someone.

"You'll be warmer when we get inside," he whispered to her, his breath tickling her ear. "How far is it?"

"Building G is right there." She pointed to the looming hulk of the four-story office building at the west-most corner of the business complex, which sat next to Building H.

"That's J. Callaway Insurance?"

"No, my workplace is Building H. Building G is empty right now, but both buildings used to be used by the Jorden Corporation. My card key will get us into Building G, and there's a walkway on the fourth floor that will get us into Building H."

"They won't see us entering Building G?"

"We'll use the back entrance, which can't be seen from the parking lot."

"Let's start avoiding the lampposts." He steered her onto the grass, wet and sharp with cold dew.

They melted into the shadows as they approached the entrance doors, which were lighted by an overhead floodlight. The light couldn't be avoided, but Jane swiped her card key quickly through the card reader and the bolts for the door snapped open. She yanked at the glass door and they slipped inside.

He headed to the elevator doors in the foyer, but Jane pulled him to the stairwell. "The elevators are really slow. It's faster to walk up."

They climbed to the fourth floor, their steps echoing loudly in the spartan stairwell. She led him through a large area empty of anything but shabby looking cubicles to the far corridor that ended at another locked door. She swiped her card and got them access to the enclosed walkway to Building H.

They walked quickly, but Jane glanced down to where she could see a corner of the parking lot. There were no cars, but anyone after them could have parked in a dark corner of the lot that she couldn't see.

Building H had more carpeting than empty Building G, but it created a muffled pall that made Jane nervous. Anyone could sneak up on them.

"Where to?" he asked.

"Second floor."

They took the stairwell down two flights to the IT department, one room filled with servers and another office area where her cubicle sat against a wall. The air was cold and dry from the air conditioning keeping the equipment from overheating in the server room, and she could hear the whir of the fans. She didn't turn on the lights, however, as she made her way to her desk.

Like her dining room table at home, her desk was piled with papers as well as equipment and cables, almost burying her desktop computer. She picked up the phone. "I have to call Security to let them know I'm here."

"Aren't they in the building?"

"No, Security is across campus in Building A, but they'll have seen my card key entry already on their computer monitors."

He nodded, but his eyes were moving around the quiet room at her coworkers' desks.

Jane dialed Security, and a friendly man's voice answered immediately. "Hi, Miss Lawton. I saw your card key entry through Building G."

"Hi, James." She always chatted with James and it would look strange if she didn't, so she said, "You got the night shift again this week?"

He gave a long-suffering sigh. "Yup. Jesse's got the flu. But the overtime will pay for a new bike for my daughter."

"How's Rosa's broken arm? Did she get her cast off yet?"

"It comes off next week."

"Bet she can't wait." She saw Alex's wary expression. "James, I'm not sure how long I'll be here tonight."

"No problem, Miss Lawton. When you do leave, just to warn you, a couple hours ago, I got an error message from the card key reader for the front door of Building G. I went to check it, and it looked okay, but let me know if you have problems."

"All right. Thanks, James."

As she hung up the phone, a chill passed through her that had nothing to do with the darkness, or the air conditioning. An error message for the card key reader … and they'd made noise walking down the stairwell … and she'd spent time chatting with James …

The air in her lungs suddenly felt thin.

"Alex—"

He turned toward her.

The gunshot was deafening, even with the carpet and cloth-covered cubicle walls absorbing some of the sound. His entire body jerked. "Jane, get down!"

Her scream lodged in her throat. She fell to her knees beside him, her shaking hands pressing to the dark, wet stain on his arm. It felt hot to the touch, or maybe her hands were cold.

If he hadn't turned toward her at that moment, where would he have been shot instead?

His body jolted at the pressure of her hands on his wound. "They're coming for you," he said through gritted teeth.

No, they were coming for the computer. She had an idea.

"Put pressure on it." She guided his hand to the wound, then moved to her desk. She reached for a hammer and an extra laptop hard drive. She hadn't removed the hard drive from the laptop yet, but they didn't know that.

"Stay back or I'll destroy the hard drive!"

She peeked around the edge of her cubicle wall and saw two men in the shadows of the door to the office room. One was the man who had been on the fire escape balcony. She got a better look at him this time, noting his dark hair, dark skin, wiry build, and the gun he held in his hand. His nose had been broken in his fight with Alex, and there was already dark purple bruising beneath his eye.

The second man was a stranger to her, but she remembered Alex's description of the finely dressed man at the meth lab. This man wore a polo shirt and slacks, and he didn't have a gun. When he turned his head, she saw he was wearing glasses.

"You're being ridiculous, Jane," the Glasses Man called to her, but he didn't come any closer. "You're trapped."

After tracking Alex to her apartment, he must have gone through it to find out who she was. "Trapped animals are the most vicious," she shot back. "I have a hammer and your hard drive here on my desk."

"Well, that's convenient," he drawled. He even stuck his hands in his pants pockets. "You work in IT, Jane. Of course you'd have extra hard drives lying around. That one isn't mine."

"Are you so sure about that? The hard drive was a breeze compared to when I removed your bluetooth card and wireless adapter." She rattled off the specs of the pieces she had removed earlier this evening. "Those are yours, aren't they?"

She could see that the Glasses Man had stiffened. "Jane, you can't win. As soon as I saw your apartment, as soon as I found out what you do for a living, I knew you'd come here, to your workplace, to utilize your computers here."

"He's just trying to rattle you. Don't listen to him." Alex's whisper was right next to her ear, and she jumped. He had gotten up and was crouched next to her, blood still slowly soaking into his shirtsleeves.

"Your arm——"

"I'm fine. I have an idea. Keep him talking." He grabbed the fire extinguisher she kept under her desk and silently moved away, staying low and under the edge of the cubicles so the two men couldn't see him. The thick carpet muffled his footsteps.

"Jane, I got into a locked building just to wait for you. And no one will be able to find any evidence at the card key reader that we were here. They might even think you let us into the building. Do you see? There's nothing I can't do." Glasses Man nodded to his associate, who started moving toward the far wall.

Her heart rate picked up. Would he be able to see Alex? "One more step, and I'm going to start whaling on this hard drive."

The man didn't stop walking.

"You can't blame me for knowing Alex is somewhere planning something," Glasses Man said, "gunshot wound or not."

"I'm sure you could retrieve *some* data from isolated sectors in a broken platter," Jane said, "but not much."

Glasses Man's face became an ugly sneer, then he hissed at his associate, who finally stopped moving.

After a moment, Glasses Man regained his confident, almost-bored tone. "What are we doing to do, Jane? Sit here all night?"

Maybe she could play the stupid female role. "Your friend is going to drop his gun, and then I'm going to throw the hard drive to you."

Even in the darkness of the office, she could see Glasses Man smile. "Fine. And then we'll let you both go. No harm, no foul."

Yeah, right. "Okay." She tried not to let her sarcasm show.

Glasses Man nodded to his associate, who reluctantly set his gun on the floor close to his foot.

"Kick it away from you," Jane said.

The man frowned, but nudged the gun away a few inches with his foot. If she told him to kick it farther, he might take a step and see Alex, wherever he was.

Jane slowly stood up so the two men could see her over the top of the cubicle walls. She raised the hard drive in her left hand, while her right still clenched tightly around the hammer. "Here it is."

"Just throw it to me nice and easy," Glasses Man said.

Jane stepped out so that she had a clear line of sight to Glasses Man. She made as if to throw the hard drive, then hurled the hammer straight at his knees.

At that moment, Alex leaped up and shot the other man with a blast from the fire extinguisher. The sound roared in Jane's ears.

Her hammer struck Glasses Man's left kneecap. He crumpled, but his shout of pain was drowned by the report from the other man's gun.

Alex! Was he all right?

Jane dropped to the ground. She hesitated, but knew what Alex would want her to do. She began crawling frantically toward the door. She was tempted to get to her feet, but didn't want to become a target for the other man and his gun.

Glasses Man lay rolling on the floor and she had to circle wide around him. However, he lunged for her and grabbed her ankle. His face was contorted with rage and pain, and his fingers bit into her tendons and bones.

She pulled her other foot back and kicked at him, but his head was too far away, so she began aiming for his elbow. She slammed into it once, then twice. Finally his hand loosened and she yanked her ankle free.

He swore at her and lunged for her again, both hands scrabbling at her legs.

God, help me!

At that moment, she spotted a dark shape on the beige carpet. The hammer, where it had fallen after it ricocheted off of the man's knee. She dove for it, her fingers curling around the smooth wooden handle. She twisted around and swung it wildly at the man's hands.

He jerked his hands back, but the hammer knocked at a finger or knuckle, and he winced.

And then suddenly a huge figure crashed on top of Glasses Man, rolling them away.

"Alex!"

Alex swung a fist at the man's jaw, and his eyes rolled back, showing the whites. His body immediately became a rag doll.

Jane crawled to him at the same moment he looked up at her. "Are you all right?" they both asked at the same time.

And then Jane's hands were around his waist, her head tucked under his chin, his arms tight around her. His heartbeat galloped under her cheek, and she felt the *whoosh* of his hard breathing. The scent of his musk wrapped around her like a cape.

It was only for a few seconds, a handful of heartbeats. He released her. "I knocked the other one out, but it won't be long before they come to."

She nodded, and forced herself to her shaky legs. She stumbled back to her desk to grab the messenger bag with the laptop, then followed him out of the building.

They ran back to the car, slipping over the cold grass, their breaths faint white puffs in the air. Once inside, she gunned the engine and shot back down the residential street they'd followed to get to the business complex.

Her hands shook, and she tightened them against the steering wheel. It took her a while to realize Alex was calling her name.

"Jane. Jane, slow down."

Her jaw was clamped shut, so she inhaled sharply through her nose. As she exhaled, she eased up on the accelerator, then finally stepped on the brakes. They stopped in the middle of a lonely stretch of road under a large oak tree. Shadows enveloped the car.

His hand covered hers on the steering wheel. His palm was tacky. It took her a moment to realize it was his blood.

"We need to take you to a hospital," she said.

He shook his head. "It's only a flesh wound."

"Men always say that in the movies."

She saw the gleam of his teeth as he smiled. "This time, it really is. Trust me, I've been shot before. Besides, the hospital will have to report the gunshot wound."

"We have to clean it." She considered her cousin Monica Grant, who was a nurse by profession, but she didn't want to involve her family in something so dangerous. Besides which, Monica still lived at home with their Aunt Becca, who happened to be dating Detective Carter. It wouldn't be the best thing to run into him with a man bleeding from a gunshot wound.

And she couldn't forget the laptop. There was only one option she could think of, and it caused a violent twisting in her gut. She screwed her eyes shut, leaning her head back against the headrest. It couldn't be avoided. He needed help, and she needed that computer equipment.

She put the car in motion again.

"Where are we going?"

"The only place I know where we can clean your wound and find a computer to analyze the hard drive." She swallowed the bitter bile that rose up in her throat. "We're going to my parents' house."

5

Jane hadn't spoken to her father since that day, over a year ago. Even worse than what Derek and done to her had been the carelessness of her father's words, which had cut like her grandfather's *katana* sword thrust into her heart.

Taking back roads all the way, Jane and Alex drove into her parents' neighborhood just as the sun turned the sky to pale orange. Jane knew they'd already be awake.

Just go in, use her dad's computer. He wouldn't refuse her, especially not with a guest present. If he said anything to her, she could just ignore it.

She no longer cared about earning his good opinion.

They didn't drive right up to her parents' house, just in case the Tumibays were watching the front. Instead, she took a different street that wound its way through some foothills before curving back around to edge the property behind her parents' home. They parked along the side of the road next to a ditch and a fence.

When she got out of her car, a ray of morning sun kissed her cheek, and she paused, closing her eyes and feeling the gentle warmth. A lot had happened to her in the past year, and she'd spent time dealing with it. But now, she wondered if maybe she was ready to move on, for new beginnings.

Her gaze slid to Alex, who had climbed out of the tiny car and was stretching his long body. Just a few hours in his company, and she was starting to release her pain. How did he do that?

They hopped the fence, then crossed the pasture, smelling strongly of cow, to a second fence that bordered the backyard of the Lawton family home. The wide swatch of manicured grass had a flagstone border along the sides, and Jane walked slowly, noticing that the leaves of her mother's miniature rose bushes, lining the walkway, were a pale, mottled green because of the cold weather. She climbed the two short steps to the covered back porch. With a quick indrawn breath, she knocked on the back door.

Her mother answered, dressed in an apron. Rather than being surprised that her daughter knocked on the back instead of the front door, she had a slightly vague smile on her face. "Jane, what a surprise."

"Hi, Mom." Jane had to bend almost double to kiss her tiny mother's cheek.

"You're just in time for breakfast." Her mother's dark eyes drifted onto Alex, standing behind Jane, his head almost brushing the roof of the porch. He'd draped his jacket in such a way that it hid the bloody stain on his shirt.

"Mom, you remember Alex Villa? Edward's brother."

He smiled at her mother as if Jane's introduction had not been as stiff as a dead tree. "We met at Edward and Rachel's engagement party, Mrs. Lawton."

"Yes, now I remember. Well, I suppose you should come in." She turned and led the way inside.

Jane steeled herself before she crossed the threshold, as if there were some invisible barrier she had to fight through. She felt Alex's hand touching the small of her back, and turned to look at him.

His face registered more concern than curiosity. He didn't ask meaningless questions like if she was all right, because he could see that she wasn't, but he said in a low voice, "I'm right here."

The words rumbled beneath her breastbone, an oasis of calmness, a source of strength.

The back door opened into the laundry room, which in turn led to the kitchen. Her father sat at the breakfast table, reading the morning paper.

"Hi, Dad," Jane said neutrally. She knew he'd heard their conversation when Mom answered the door.

He grunted but didn't look at her, continuing to read his paper.

"Dad, this is Alex Villa."

He treated her friend like an extension of Jane, simply frowning and nodding curtly to Alex, before returning to his paper.

Yes, he was still upset at the words she'd flung at him the last time they'd spoken, over a year ago. Maybe she was more like him than she realized, because wasn't she still holding a grudge, too?

"Mrs. Lawton, could I use your bathroom?" Alex asked.

"Oh, certainly." She waved toward the hallway.

"I'll show you." Jane led the way out of the kitchen, but she detoured into the extra bedroom that had used to belong to her. She knew her mom still kept some of her brother's old clothes in the dresser, and she grabbed a knit polo shirt that would stretch to fit Alex. She gestured toward the hallway bathroom and whispered, "First Aid kit is under the sink."

He nodded and went to clean his wound.

"Scrambled eggs okay?" Her mom was at the stove, melting butter. It sizzled, and Jane realized how hungry she was.

Years of habit made her look to her father's face for signs of his opinion. He wasn't looking at her, but he wasn't frowning, so she said, "Yes. Thanks, Mom."

"Did you want some coffee?" Her mother nodded toward the coffeemaker on the counter.

Jane retrieved mugs from the cabinet and poured coffee for herself and Alex. By the time she finished, the toast had popped up in the toaster, so she put them on a plate and buttered them for her mom. She took the toast to the kitchen table along with some plates for everyone just as Alex returned from the bathroom. Neither of her parents seemed to notice the different shirt, which was a little snug on his large frame.

She and Alex sat at the table to sip coffee and munch on toast, and her father finally spoke up, without putting down his paper. "You don't have food at your own house?" Implied was the criticism that she had to come to her parents' house to get fed.

Or was she reading more into it than was there? She wasn't about to address her parental issues with Alex here. "Dad, could I use your computer? I have a hard drive I want to access."

"Where's yours?"

"Inaccessible," she replied in the same clipped tone he had used.

The paper lowered so he could regard her with a pale blue eye beneath his bushy gray brows. "What's that supposed to mean?"

"Exactly that, Dad."

"Please." Mom laid a plate of scrambled eggs on the table. "Don't fight."

Jane backed down, and her father went back to reading his paper. She spooned eggs on her toast and finished eating it before saying, "May I please use your computer, Dad?"

He didn't reply.

Jane took a last sip of coffee. "If you'd rather I didn't, we'll just go." She stood up, and Alex followed suit.

"I didn't say that," her father said irritably. He jerked his head toward his office. "Go ahead. You know the password."

Jane suspected that he'd only agreed so he wouldn't look quite so churlish in front of Alex, but she didn't care. She headed to the living room, followed by Alex's silent form, and went through to the hallway. At the end of the short corridor was the open door to his office.

Jane was struck by how much it resembled her dining room table. She'd never noticed before. She and Alex sat at two chairs in front of her father's computer, and she took out the laptop. She shoved some papers and equipment aside to have room to set it on the desk.

He surprised her with a warm hand gently massaging the tight muscles at the base of her neck. He didn't say anything, but his touch was reassuring, pouring cold water on her sizzling temper.

She paused to take a deep breath. She didn't look at him, but she touched his hand with her fingers once. Then she went to work.

She knew where to rummage in her father's desk for his screwdrivers and other small instruments she needed to open up the laptop and remove the hard drive. It was a bit tricky because a few components had been taped down, and she had to remove the tape carefully.

She was just finishing when her father wandered into his office, coffee cup in hand. He peered over her shoulder at the laptop on the desk. "Whose is that?"

"No one you know." Jane lifted the drive from the casing.

"Why are *you* fiddling with it?"

"Alex knew I could handle the security software measures."

He grunted. He'd been in IT until he retired, and his company had often looked to him for computer security questions. "Someone locked themselves out of their computer?"

"I have to bypass the security software or this data will be as good as lost."

"You didn't do something stupid like try to turn it on, did you?"

"No, Dad," Jane said through a clenched jaw.

"Because if there's security software loaded directly into the UEFI, the computer could just connect to the internet to receive instructions. It might erase everything before you get a chance to try to get in."

Which was exactly what she'd told Alex, back in Jorge's tavern. "That's why I removed the wireless adapter, Dad. And the Bluetooth card for good measure."

He peered at the open laptop casing. "You did a messy job removing that Bluetooth card."

Was it her imagination, or was he more critical of her since their argument? For most of her life, she'd have done anything to prove herself to him, to win the same kind of approval that he doled out to her older brother so freely.

But now, more than ever, she was aware of how his criticism felt like hammer blows, knocking her down.

Alex interrupted him. "Mr. Lawton, how's your son doing?" His voice was tight, but polite.

One of Dad's favorite topics. That should keep him off of Jane's back for a little while. She flashed Alex a grateful look for distracting her father.

Dad's voice took on a brighter note. "Jason's company went IPO last year, you heard about that? He and his wife bought a new house in Cupertino."

She hooked up the hard drive to her father's computer and wasn't surprised to see full-disk encryption. However, she had probably bypassed the laptop's tracking software.

Her father listed the specs of a new tablet computer that Jason's company had just released, which probably bored Alex to tears, but to his credit, he kept a politely interested expression on his face as her father talked.

Jane worked steadily. She'd heard about all this from Jason himself. Her brother truly was brilliant, if arrogant, and Jane's relationship with him hadn't been altered by her tension with their father. Jason and his wife had Jane over for dinner once a month or so, and he kept urging Jane to quit her low-paying IT job to write software for his company. Jane had considered it, but the idea of working for her brother had seemed suffocating, as if she were still working for Derek's company, EMRY. Jason would demand everything he could from her—he would use her, like Derek had.

She made a working copy of the hard drive and then started attacking the encryption with various programs and scripts. She didn't look at Alex very often. He mostly sat beside her and listened to her father. But she started to sense the tension in his muscles. His hands clenched and unclenched once or twice. His leg jiggled every so often. When she did glance at him, she noticed the hard line of his jaw.

Was he frustrated at her lack of progress? She couldn't help it. This wasn't a run-of-the-mill laptop used for emails and web surfing.

Or was he trying not to be bored to death by her dad's going on about his perfect son?

"You must be proud at how successful Jason has become," Alex said to her father. There was a strange, hard edge to his voice that Jane didn't understand. She glanced at him, but beyond a glitter in his dark eyes and the rigid set of his shoulders, nothing seemed amiss.

Her father chuckled. "He's smart, but he's worked hard, too—"

"Both your children are pretty smart."

Jane winced. Her vertebrae fused together as she tried not to anticipate her father's reply. They were only words.

Dad snorted. "This one doesn't have what it takes to make it in the high tech business." He then noticed when she opened a program she'd written specifically for her work at EMRY. "What are you doing? That program is trying to force a volume to mount."

"I've looked through the visible volume, but I think there's a hidden partition."

"Why aren't you just breaking the encryption?"

"I might lose some data."

"Sure, but the hidden partition will be fine. *If* there is one."

Jane's temper flared. "There's nothing there. If it were me, I would have at least one hidden partition unmounted at all times for my most sensitive data. We need to get everything off this hard drive."

"Why do you … Wait a minute."

Oh, no. She had said too much.

"What exactly are you doing?" His voice rose. "I thought you were just trying to help someone who locked themselves out of their computer."

"Dad, I don't have time to explain—"

"You better find time to explain."

"All I can tell you is that it's important." Jane's typing grew harder and faster on the keyboard.

"Important? What kind of trouble have you gotten yourself into?"

"I'm not in trouble."

"No? Then why are you breaking into someone's hard drive?" he roared.

She squeezed her eyes shut in frustration. "There's more to it than that—"

"This is rich, coming from you." His voice had grown hard and vicious. "After all the stuff you spouted about Derek and EMRY. I bet you're regretting your bad decision now."

"It wasn't a bad decision," she said hoarsely.

"Your problem is you think nobody knows better than yourself."

She wanted to laugh and scream at the same time. He'd exactly described himself.

"Blayne," her mother's voice called from the living room. "Your blood pressure ..."

"I'm just telling my daughter what she needs to hear. She's never going to learn if she doesn't hear it straight from someone."

There was an almost audible *snap!* in her head. Never going to learn. It was true. She had been denying it her entire life. She'd thought she could learn how to please him. But the reality was that she would never have his approval. *That* was the lesson she'd needed to learn.

The words shot out of her mouth. "I am not your daughter. I'm some puppy you like to kick around."

There was a horrible moment of silence.

Then her mother's wheedling voice, "Blayne ..."

Jane kept typing, but she heard her father leave his office.

Then the soft words from her mother reached her ears. "Leave her alone. You need to let her make her own mistakes."

Something squeezed hard inside of her. It choked her. She couldn't breathe, but she didn't care.

The slamming of her father's office door made her jerk in her seat. She gasped in a breath, and her heartbeat roared hard and fast in her ears. She twisted around to see Alex locking the door.

"You can't lock my dad out of his own office," she said feebly.

"I just did." He began pacing—more like prowling—in front of the door, his mouth hard and his eyes fierce. "Are you almost done?"

She turned back to the computer. "Sort of. The program did

find a hidden partition and I'm running another piece of software to retrieve data from the exposed sectors." Her voice was rising as she babbled. "I'm working as fast as——"

"Jane." His gentle voice and the soft pressure of his hands on her shoulders made her feel as if her heart had cracked open. She swallowed.

And then he was sitting beside her, taking her hands in his. "Jane, I wasn't rushing you. I want to leave because I can't stand listening to him talk to you that way."

She began to tremble, and his fingers pressed harder against her palms.

No one had ever protected her against her father.

"He's not always this caustic," she was forced to admit. "It's only been in the last year that he's gotten like this." Before that, she had always responded eagerly to his instructions, so he had no need to be scornful. But after quitting her job at EMRY, she had become the arrogant, foolish daughter, and so was treated as such. "And I couldn't explain to him about the hard drive, so that frustrated him."

"Don't defend him," he said fiercely, which surprised her. "He's your father. He shouldn't speak to you that way."

Jane realized that Alex's hands were trembling now, too.

The computer beeped, and she pulled her hands away to get back to her work. She blinked at the screen. "I don't understand."

"What?"

"It's done."

"Isn't that a good thing?"

"Sort of ... It took less time than I thought it would." She frowned and double-checked that the software had done its job. "Let's go. I sent the data packets to my secure cloud drive." She started packing up, including the copy of the hard drive that she had made. She spotted a laptop made by her brother's company and grabbed it.

He unlocked the door and they exited the office. Jane said stiffly, "Dad, I'm going to borrow this laptop, if you're not using it?" She held it up.

He barely looked at her. He sat on the living room couch, frowning fiercely, his face a splotchy red. "Fine."

"Thanks. I'll return it."

Neither of her parents said anything as she and Alex crossed the living room to the open doorway into the kitchen.

"Thanks for breakfast, Mr. and Mrs. Lawton." Alex strode into the kitchen and out the back door as if escaping from jail.

Jane hesitated in the doorway, as she had when she first entered the threshold. Her head bowed. She opened her mouth, then closed it. What was there to say? "Bye." She left.

They crossed the field again in silence. Cows were grazing at a distance, and the animals gave them uninterested looks as they climbed over the fence.

She always felt … efficient when she got into her hybrid car. But today, she remembered her father convincing her to buy it.

She was done pleasing her father.

She should have felt empowered, free. Instead she felt weighted down and unwieldy, like when she'd had to move an old-fashioned tube computer monitor and the large, heavy thing had nearly taken her arms off at the sockets.

As she drove back down the road, he asked, "Are you all right?"

"As fine as I can be." That wasn't true. She felt alone. She felt as if she'd always been alone.

And what had all that gotten for them? "I think there's something wrong with the hard drive."

A vein in his temple pulsed. "Wrong, how?"

"The security on the drive was relatively minimal."

"Maybe he got lazy about security. No one ever expects their computer to go missing."

"Maybe. Or maybe the information on the hard drive isn't as important as we thought." She glanced at him, nervous about conveying her fears. "What if there isn't any proof that the Tumibays set you up? What if there's nothing to convict the Tumibays of any crimes?" She swallowed. "What if all this was for nothing?"

"It's not for nothing." He put strong emphasis on his words, but

Jane heard a thread of determination. Or desperation. "What do we need now?"

"I need internet access so we can look at the files on my cloud drive. I thought maybe we could go back to Jorge's tavern to use his internet." She turned onto the main road that led out of her parents' neighborhood.

"No, there will be lots of people at the tavern by now, and we don't know who might belong to the Tumibays." He was silent a moment, then he heaved a sigh. "I know where we can get wireless internet easily. The only problem is that ..."

They were passing a blue Dodge Challenger heading in the opposite direction, and it wasn't until they were almost next to each other that Jane recognized the driver.

The man from the fire escape balcony. And in the passenger seat, the polo shirt man.

6

Jane slammed on the gas.

The Challenger's tires squealed as the two men turned to follow them.

Jane's heart was drumming, her hands on the steering wheel trembled. The hybrid car had no chance against the Challenger. It was only a matter of time before the more powerful car caught up to them.

She had to even the odds.

"Jane, traffic." Alex's voice was tight, his hands white knuckled as he gripped the dashboard. "You need traffic."

There was a large shopping mall nearby. This main road led toward it, but there was also Barclay Road, a narrow, winding road that led to the southeast side of the mall. And she knew a shortcut to it.

Jane made a sudden left turn into a long dirt driveway. The Challenger had been too close, and they overshot the driveway. In the time it took them to swerve and follow them, Jane was nearly at the end of the driveway, coming up to the farmhouse. The car skidded sideways on the dirt as she turned right onto a farm road that would cut her through the farm property to Barclay Road.

The Challenger's engine roared. The men were within a car's length of her back bumper when Jane flew out of the farm road, jouncing up onto the asphalt as she turned onto Barclay Road.

As a teen, she had often loved driving this winding road at dangerous speeds, and she pulled out all the stops now. The road was narrower than a residential street, with sharp turns that rolled up and down. The hybrid caught air as she drove over the top of a rise, crashing down with a bounce that made her teeth clack together.

She didn't want to take her eyes off the road. "Are they gaining on us?"

He had twisted around. "No. But they're not falling behind."

Jane went faster.

Barclay Road finally T-junctioned with Lewis Expressway, a broad road that would take them past the mall and eventually onto the freeway. Jane took a hard right onto the expressway, directly in front of an oncoming minivan. She left the sound of the minivan's horns behind them as she accelerated as fast as the hybrid could handle.

As she had during the escape from her apartment, she wove in between cars aggressively. The expressway didn't have a wide enough shoulder for the Challenger to drive on it to catch up to them. But she needed to lose their pursuers, not just get ahead of them.

She cut sharply across two lanes into a left turn lane, then jammed in front of the oncoming cars. Tires squealed. Car horns blared in a cacophony directly into her ears as they shot down a side road.

"Did they follow us?"

"No, they couldn't. But they'll be trying to find a way back to find us again."

This road led to another residential area, with farms. She remembered that there was one family who had horses—and a large barn.

She took a few turns, including a shortcut through a small orchard, following the dirt tractor trail. She finally saw the barn coming up on her left, and turned into the driveway. The house of the family who owned the property was far enough away from the barn that they wouldn't notice if she parked behind it, which would hide their car from view of the road.

When Jane turned off the engine, she gasped as if she hadn't taken a breath the entire frightening time.

"You're okay." He clenched her hand in his. "You did great. They weren't behind us from the moment you made that left turn."

His touch was hot, spreading warmth down her hands, into her wrists. She unclamped her fingers from around the steering wheel, and he let go.

She massaged her cramped fingers. "How did they find us?"

"I think this was by accident. They were heading toward your parent's house."

"But I thought they might have already been watching the house."

"Maybe we gave them too much credit. It might have taken them this long to guess you might go to your parents' place. Or maybe they did have someone in front of their house, and those two were coming to relieve them."

Jane heaved a sigh and leaned her head back against the head rest. "We need a new car."

"We need to look through the data you pulled from the hard drive. And I think I know where we can do both."

Alex looked around, making sure there was no one in sight as he and Jane crossed the strip of forested land between the neighboring farm's access road and the east edge of his brother's property. The nearest greenhouse lay only a few yards from the treeline.

They approached the frosted door, and he grasped the handle. It turned easily in his hand.

"You said this was dangerous?" Jane asked him as they entered the greenhouse.

"Not for us, for me." He sighed heavily. "My brother is going to kill me."

Edward stood leaning against a stainless steel gardening table, arms crossed, his face like thunder. Luckily, Mama was nowhere to be seen.

Edward noticed him looking around. "Don't worry, I didn't tell Mama."

"Praise God for small blessings."

Edward spotted Jane, and his grim expression softened. He came forward to kiss her cheek. "Hi, Jane. Are you all right?"

"I'm fine." Even with little sleep, her smile for his brother was wide, and her eyes turned to amber in the sunlight slanting through the glass panes on the roof. She was still a little pale from her ordeal with her father.

While at her parents' house, Alex had had to fight to keep his big mouth shut in order to be respectful, but he'd wanted to jump up to defend her every time the man grated out yet another harsh observation of his daughter, another worshipful tidbit about his son. The man was toxic, and while he might have gotten worse only in the last year, as Jane had said, there was something about his manner to Jane that made it obvious that he was rarely complimentary.

Alex's father had not been kind, and he had been stubborn, but he had rarely been cruel. Alex couldn't imagine what that kind of relationship had done to Jane's self-esteem. Maybe that was also why her faith had seemed to have become lukewarm lately.

"You're lucky I don't give you a thrashing," Edward said to him.

"What do you mean? I left a message on your phone yesterday."

"'I don't know how long I'll be gone, don't freak out if I don't answer my cell phone, and protect Mama'? You call that a message?"

Jane bit her lip to hide her smile, and the shadow of a dimple appeared in her left cheek.

"All this after you'd been arrested a few days ago," Edward continued. "Your communication skills suck, bro."

"I was distracted," he said. "I was trying to lose a tail."

Edward's dark brows slammed down over his eyes. "You better explain that."

He told him everything, which only made his brother more and more alarmed.

"You got shot? Why didn't you tell me that when you called?" Edward stepped forward, scanning Alex's body. "Where?"

He winced as he eased off his jacket, then rolled up the sleeve of the borrowed shirt. "Grazed me."

Edward wasn't so blasé. "You idiot. That needs to be taken care of. Stitches, or—"

"I will." He'd been shot before on more than one occasion, and although his arm hurt, this wasn't as bad as some other wounds he'd had. He needed stitches, but he also knew he could get away with waiting before he had it looked at. He'd used butterfly bandages to close the wound, which had stopped bleeding, at least.

Jane said, "I just realized there are at least two bullet holes in the walls of the IT office at my workplace."

"Maybe your coworkers won't notice?" Alex said.

"You're going to tell Detective Carter all about it," Edward said firmly. "I don't understand why you didn't speak to him about this first."

"His superiors are not happy that he defended me," he said. "I didn't want to involve him until I had proof that I was innocent."

"Because everything you've done so far has made you seem above suspicion?"

"Alex wasn't the one coming after us with guns," Jane said quietly.

Edward sighed, then tapped the computer lying on the table next to him. "I brought my laptop, as you asked."

"Good. Jane has another one, so we can both look through the data from that hard drive."

"There's WiFi here?" Jane looked around the greenhouse. It was only partially filled at the moment with the last of the latest Malaysian basil crop that Edward and Alex were growing for Rachel Grant. It certainly didn't look like an internet cafe.

"All the greenhouses have WiFi," Edward said. "The buildings have security and sensors, and Alex helped me install soil sensors for the plants. We needed WiFi to be able to monitor them all with our computers." Edward hesitated, then said, "Is there anything else I can do?"

"Do me a favor," he said, "and don't tell——"

"I won't tell Mama," Edward said. "But just ..." His mouth tightened, and his expression was anguished. "... Just fix this. Soon."

He nodded.

Edward cleared his throat and clumsily waved a hand toward a paper sack on the table. "I made you sandwiches, and there's bottled water and a thermos of coffee."

"Thanks." His head was starting to whirl from lack of sleep. He'd be glad for food and more caffeine. He hadn't been able to eat much at Jane's parents' house.

"Have you slept at all?"

"After the car chase, since we were out of sight of the road, we napped in the car for a couple hours." Then they'd been awakened by the farmer whose land they were parked on, demanding they leave his property.

Edward's cell phone beeped once, and he glanced at it. "I have to get back to work." Edward gave him a long, steady look, then left the greenhouse.

He grabbed two stools and set them at the gardening table. The greenhouses were all equipped with electrical outlets which had covers to protect them from water when there wasn't anything plugged in, so they had power for the laptops. After he had connected them to the WiFi, Jane told him how to access her cloud drive, and divided up the data she'd retrieved from the hard drive.

They worked in silence for a few minutes. He glanced at her intent face a few times. Finally he said, "Did you want to talk about it?"

"No." Her jaw tightened briefly.

"Jane, you can't pretend you don't feel anything." He had learned that lesson very well.

"It's none of your business. You shouldn't have witnessed that in the first place."

"I think I witnessed that for a reason. I think I understand better than you realize."

She sighed, bowing her head and rubbing her forehead with her fingers. "He's not normally like that. It's only been for the past year."

She had mentioned that before. "What happened last year?"

Her face hardened, and her voice was hollow as she said, "I quit my job, and Dad thought it was a bad idea."

"Why did you quit? You loved your job."

"It didn't love me." There was something odd in her tone as she said that. Something bruised.

"Jane—"

"Alex, just leave it alone."

"Look, I get it. I get not living up to your father's expectations." He couldn't stop his hands from clenching as he said it. After all these years, it still stabbed at him like a broken bone that wouldn't heal properly.

Jane had stilled. The silence hung between them like the heavy chill at the bottom of a canyon. Finally she whispered, "It never occurred to me that you and Edward never talk about him."

"The last time I spoke to my father, was an argument the week before I got arrested."

"But ... he died after you got out of prison."

"Don't get me wrong, he had every reason to yell at me. I ran with a bad crowd. I'd been bullied in grade school, so when I filled out, I vowed to protect anyone else who got bullied, but some of them were into things I should have avoided. After high school, I got even worse. That's what Papa and I argued about."

He could still hear the thundering of his father's voice, shuddering off the walls of the low-ceilinged living room. He heard Mama's pleas. Papa's normally immaculate work suit had become rumpled with the force of his anger.

"But when you became a Christian in prison ..." Jane's face was utterly confused.

"I went to him. I apologized. I told him I was a different person." His father's face had been stone. He hadn't looked at Alex. The silence had been unbearable, and Alex had finally left. "But he couldn't forgive me for the shame I'd brought on the family. On *him.*"

Her small hand reached out to cover his. The feather-light touch was like the striking of a gong, causing a deep hum throughout his body.

"When he was in the hospital, he still wouldn't speak to me. And then he died."

Jane didn't try to tell him that his father had loved him. She understood how impossible that could be to believe.

"He was disappointed in me. He simply didn't care about Edward," he said. "He abandoned both of us emotionally. So Edward and I found a father's love in God, instead."

Jane withdrew her hand and turned her face away from him. "I feel like God has abandoned me. And don't try to tell me that He hasn't, because it really feels like He has."

She sat stiffly on the stool, self-contained, brittle, and alone. He wanted to reach out to her, but he could sense that if he did, she might shatter. And he'd lose any chance at helping her.

Then words tumbled out of his mouth, and he didn't understand why he said them. "Sometimes when we feel alone, we're really not. We just can't see Him behind us."

She wrapped her arms around herself and didn't answer.

"Jane, I'll be here for you." He realized how deeply he meant it. He had always liked her, always been attracted to her, but seeing her strength in the face of stress and danger made him see how amazing she really was. "And I know you don't want to hear this, but God is here for you, too. He won't turn away from you."

"He already did." She heaved a long breath that sounded like dry leaves rattling in the orchard. "I don't want to talk about it."

He had to be content with that. *Lord, only You can convince her of how intensely You love her, of how she's not alone.*

Jane turned back to her computer. "Let's just get back to work."

It was true, he needed to clear his name. He needed to stop the

Tumibays from gaining a foothold here in Sonoma. But now, repairing his reputation was no longer as important as repairing the pain he'd seen in Jane's eyes. When this was over, he had to show her how her father was wrong.

Nothing. There was no evidence that the Tumibays had set Alex up.

He had been so sure there would be something. It might not have been front and center, but it would be there. But the hard drive didn't mention anything about Alex or even the Sonoma operation. It was all banking information and shipping records. "This is everything from the hard drive?" he asked her.

"I think so." Jane rested her forehead in her hand as she stared at her laptop. "I found that hidden partition. I thought for sure there would be something in it about the money they wired to your bank account."

"There's plenty of bank accounts here, although they're all in code. Can you crack it?"

"It's not my forte. You'd need a forensic accountant to analyze all this banking information in the hidden partition, to see if it's enough to convict anyone. "

"Did you find anything else?"

"He uses a secure cloud server for his email, so I don't have the actual messages on this computer, but I can see notes he's made to himself about messages he's sent. He doesn't email many people at all, and the ones he does email, he refers to by code names."

"What names?" He moved toward her and looked over her shoulder.

"Emeril is the one he emails the most."

He gave a bark of laughter. "Not very original. I'll bet that's the bald guy I saw at the meth lab, the one cooking the drugs."

"How can you be sure?"

"I've known lots of different drug gang members. A lot of them call their chemists 'Emeril.'"

"Then there's this one, Oyster."

He felt a bubbling in his chest, like a pot about to boil over. "That's the Tumibay captain in charge of the drug operations here in Sonoma. He's referred to as Talaba, although I'm not sure if that's his real name. It means oyster in Tagalog. Any other names? Maybe this accountant emailed Tumibay officers in San Francisco."

"He emailed four other people, and he refers to them as Sleepy, Dopey, Happy, and Doc."

He groaned. "Practically every gang on the planet has members with names from the Seven Dwarves."

"There's one other name." She clicked a few folders. "It wasn't in the hidden partition, it was a memo in the outer volume. I didn't pay much attention at first because the accountant wrote it all in code words, and since it was in the outer volume, there's a good chance it's not very important. But it's the only memo with a first and last name mentioned."

She pulled up a document. "It's about payment for delivery—he refers to it as a shipment of Thighbusters."

He had to swallow a laugh. "Seriously?"

Jane shrugged. "At the bottom is a bunch of notes to himself. One is to remind himself to ask Jejomar Babingao about delivery schedules."

He straightened. "That's not a nickname or a code name. That's a real name."

"It is?" Jane clicked through and started searching for it online. "Filipino?"

"Yes."

"For everything else he used code names. He must have overlooked this one. That's probably also why it was in the unprotected outer volume."

They actually found the man on Facebook. His page was in Filipino, but Jane put it through a translation program. He worked as a customs officer for a small shipping port in the Philippines.

Shipping from the Philippines. "Jane, you hit the jackpot."

"I did?"

"The main ingredient for meth production is ephedrine. It

comes from the *ma huang* plant. Most gangs get ephedrine from Mexico, but some still smuggle it in from the Philippines."

"So this man might be involved in supplying the ephedrine for the Tumibays?"

"The FBI can follow him back to the ephedrine supply in the Philippines. We could cut off the Tumibays' drug production at the knees."

Jane frowned at him. "But even if we give this information to the FBI, this Tumibay captain has already destroyed your relationship with the Sonoma police. This information won't necessarily change that."

He hadn't realized how much he enjoyed working with Detective Carter until it was gone. He had always been friendly with people, but with Detective Carter's support, he had been able to use his friendships to help the community. To protect people. He liked doing that.

He enjoyed working with his brother and on his mother's farm. He enjoyed the physical work, even though it was tiring, and they were fortunate that they made enough of a profit to be able to hire help so the work wasn't so backbreaking.

But his work with the Sonoma PD had slowly become as much a part of his life as his other jobs.

Except that it didn't define who he was. And if he had to give up his work with Detective Carter in order to keep firm in his own personal integrity, that's what he'd do.

"My reputation isn't worth anything to me if I don't do what I can to protect this community," he said slowly. "But we're still in danger. The Tumibay captain—the oyster guy—and the accountant will still be after us because of what we know. They might have a mole in the Sonoma PD. They'll threaten our families to get to us."

She studied him, and seemed to know what he was thinking, because she said, "It's not your fault that my family and I are in danger."

But it was.

"So what do we do?" she asked.

"If that guy in the polo shirt and glasses is the accountant, he doesn't strike me as being very loyal. If we get to him, he might flip on the Tumibay captain in charge of the meth operation in Sonoma, the Oyster."

Jane shook her head. "From what he said to me at my workplace last night, he's not stupid. He reminds me …" She gave a small sigh. "He reminds me of my brother, actually. Smart and arrogant. I don't think we should assume he'll turn on his captain. We need something that'll bring both of them in."

"Then let's play to the weaknesses of a smart but arrogant man. He still wants the hard drive."

Jane started clicking on windows on her computer. "I looked at the coding for the tracking software he had on the hard drive. I think I can alter it so that if he hooks the hard drive up to another one of his computers, it will alert one of our laptops with its location."

"But that doesn't help us also get the Oyster."

She looked up at him, speculation shining in her eyes. "I think I know how to get them both."

7

In the end, it wasn't very dramatic. Jane walked up to a car parked outside her apartment and knocked on the window. She leaned against the car frame to hide her trembling knees and told the startled Filipino man who sat inside, "I want to talk to your boss."

Alex hadn't wanted her to do this, but she'd convinced him. What choice did they have? They had reached the point where their backs were to the wall. The accountant wanted three things—the hard drive, Jane, and Alex.

Jane would guess that he'd be happy to take two out of three.

The two men took the messenger bag from her before they shoved her into the back seat of the car. The smell of garlic and onions made her gag. One of them telephoned someone, speaking rapidly in Filipino, as the driver headed out of Sonoma.

They didn't bother to blindfold her. They apparently didn't care that she saw where they were taking her. Jane closed her eyes and tried not to panic at the implications of that.

It seemed they drove for a long time, past vineyards and fields, and finally down a deep gully. The only people they saw on the road were a few bikers in black leather and a lunch wagon on its way back from the midday business.

As they drove down a deeply rutted dirt track into the foothills, the wind in their faces carried the acrid scent of ammonia. Jane coughed and breathed through her mouth. Soon the road ended next to a mobile trailer. Several yards away from the trailer sat a generator and a folding table with computer equipment.

Glasses Man sat at the table, typing at another laptop, but he stopped when he saw the car. And when he spotted Jane, he smiled.

Jane shivered.

As she got out of the car, she said, "I want to make a deal." The chemical odors from the meth lab made her cough again.

"Of course you do."

The driver handed Glasses Man the messenger bag, and he dug out the laptop casing. "You did quite a hack job on this." He set it on the table.

He next removed the laptop Jane had borrowed from her father, flipping it back and forth in his hands. "This looks like it's one made by your brother's company. I think I'll keep this."

In the side pocket of the messenger bag, he found the hard drive and the wireless adapter and Bluetooth card Jane had removed from his laptop. There was nothing else.

He stared hard at Jane with black eyes glittering. "I know you made a copy of the hard drive. It's what I would do."

Jane stared back at him, and her jaw grew tight.

"I'm sure you don't want me to ask one of these men to search you for it."

She couldn't stop the shudder that passed through her. She reached under her shirt and pulled it out from where it had been lying between her waistband and lower back. "I want to meet with your captain. I want to work for him."

"And why would he want to hire you?" The man nodded to the two who had brought Jane there, and they got back in the car. In a swirl of dust and dead leaves, they executed a three point turn and left.

The grit and heat were starting to make Jane sweat even more.

She moved from the patch of direct sunlight into the shade of a bedraggled oak tree, near the folding table. "Look and see what I did. Your full-disk encryption wasn't very encrypted."

He gave her a long look. For the first time, she noticed how young he was—her age, perhaps. He had thick dark lashes that made his eyes look like they had on eyeliner.

"Why not?" He called something guttural to the trailer, and a skinny young man—barely more than a teenager—exited the lab. His dark eyes fell on Jane with a sort of hunger that had her involuntarily taking a step back. "Happy, keep an eye on her while I work."

The young man gave Jane a feral smile, and he casually pulled a handgun from the back of his jeans. He didn't point it at her. It hung almost carelessly from his twitching fingers.

Glasses Man sat at the folding table and plugged the copied hard drive into his computer.

"What's your name? Let me guess. Doc?"

"Farmboy." He gave her a bland smile. "I bring home the bacon."

Alex had probably been right. This was an accountant for the gang.

Farmboy studied the computer, and his smile widened. "I see you didn't find the second hidden partition."

She couldn't stop the surprised twitch of her shoulders.

"You're really not as smart as you think you are. Why are you even bothering trying to play with the big boys?"

Different voice, same words. But this man wasn't her father, and she no longer cared about trying to please her dad, or any man, because none of them would ever be pleased with her. It seemed she tried so hard, and she always fell short. Why bother?

But wasn't that just fulfilling what her father had always said about her?

Farmboy laughed as he looked at the code on his screen. "Oh, that's cute. You altered the tracking software. No wonder you wanted me to look at this hard drive. Too bad there isn't a random wireless internet signal out here." He swept a hand at the twisted trees and scrub brush of the wilderness around them. "Meth labs tend to annoy the neighbors, so we had to go out a little far from civilization."

She clenched her jaw at his tone.

He feigned surprise. "Did you really think that would work? While I do have wireless internet, it has security to prevent computers from hopping on. Duh. And you really thought you could work for my boss?"

The sound of a car—no, two cars coming up the pitted road drew her attention. And then she recognized the truck in front.

Oh, no. It wasn't supposed to happen like this.

The man from the fire escape balcony drove Edward's truck, which Alex had been using. Behind him was the Challenger, driven by another man. Where was Alex?

The driver got out of the truck and lifted a hand in greeting, and Happy returned the gesture.

"Where is he?" Farmboy demanded.

The driver opened the back door to the truck cab and hauled on something heavy. Alex slid off the back seat and fell into a heap on the ground. He grunted and stirred, and Jane saw the purple bruising already starting to form around his eye. His hands had been duct-taped together.

"He was trying to follow her." The driver nodded toward Jane.

Farmboy nodded. "Thought he might."

"Let me talk to your captain," Jane said. "We can still make a deal." She had to stall. This was not going the way they had planned it.

"What do you possibly have that I would want?" Farmboy gave a short laugh. "You delivered yourself to me like a Thanksgiving turkey."

"Can I eat her?" Happy leered at her.

"Go ahead and try," Jane shot at him acidly.

A growl came from Alex's form, and he sat up with a wince. "Didn't expect that to happen," he muttered.

"You're not as good a driver as your girlfriend," jeered the driver of the Challenger.

"But you're just as stupid," Farmboy said. "I looked up the make and model of your brother's truck as soon as I figured out who you were. We've been watching for it."

Jane eyed Happy's gun, then Alex's slumped figure. Nothing was going the way Alex said it would.

Alex looked up at her from where he still sat in the dirt. "Just do it."

Farmboy spun to face her. "Do what?"

Jane glared at Alex. What was he doing?

Farmboy grabbed her shoulders and shoved her back against a tree trunk. The sharp edges dug into her spine. "Do. What."

Jane closed her eyes and exhaled. Fine. She'd do it. "It's already done."

Farmboy slammed her against the tree again, blowing the air out of her lungs. Her heart was racing like an engine.

She had to gasp a few breaths before she could speak. "The laptop."

He stared at his laptop, which sat there innocuously.

"Mine," she said.

Farmboy strode to the table and flipped open her brother's laptop. The screen was flashing, while code scrolled up the screen.

"What?" He slapped the keys. "What's it doing?"

Then the code scrolling on the screen abruptly ended, and a cursor blinked next to the words, "BAILE cloud server hacked. You lose."

Within a few seconds of him opening the laptop, it suddenly went dark.

Farmboy rushed at Jane, his fingers biting into her shoulders. Happy grinned and raised his gun, and then there was the sound of guns being drawn by the other two gang members, as well. "Hey, hey!" Alex said.

From the mobile trailer, a tall man with a shaved head emerged, also holding a gun.

"Calm down or you'll never know what happened." Alex had risen to his knees, his hands still taped together, which contrasted with the ring of authority in his voice.

Farmboy's face was close to Jane's. Anger had drawn harsh lines against his mouth, alongside his nose. His breath was hot and foul in her face.

"If you hurt her, you'll never find out what she did." Alex's voice sounded reasonable and confident. "And I sure couldn't tell you."

If they got out of this alive, Jane was going to kill him. Or even worse, tell everything to his mama, and let *her* kill him.

Farmboy shoved Jane once more, but stepped back. Happy sighed and dropped his gun, and the others did, as well.

"I hacked your cloud server." Jane's throat was dry, and she swallowed.

"I know that," Farmboy bit out. "What did you do to it? How did you do it?"

"I knew you had secure WiFi at the other meth lab, because I saw the network connection on the laptop Alex stole, although I figured you'd change the password. But your second laptop would be connected to the internet, and if I could get your guys to bring me to you ..."

Farmboy paled. His lips barely moved as he said, "What did you do?"

"I uploaded a virus that hit my workplace a few weeks ago. They're all insurance guys so they weren't very cautious about spammy emails. I altered the virus." Jane licked her lips. "It's being sent specifically to your captain."

Farmboy backhanded her across the mouth. Pain shot up her jaw as if it had been disconnected, and she tasted blood. She'd bitten her tongue.

"Hey!" Alex had climbed to his feet.

The driver of the Challenger shoved his gun in Alex's face. "Get back."

"The virus," Farmboy said to her.

Jane spat out some blood. "It'll email everyone in your captain's address book, except I altered this one to carbon copy the Sonoma police department on all those emails. So the Sonoma PD will see every person your captain has ever contacted." It hurt for her to talk.

Farmboy whipped out his cell phone, and within seconds he was talking to someone in Filipino. He repeated himself earnestly a few times, then his brow clouded in confusion.

Was it enough time? Had her program worked?

Finally he hung up the phone, then stalked to Jane. "He didn't get an email. You didn't do anything."

"Of course not—"

He drew back his hand. Alex yelled, "Hey!"

Jane cringed and quickly said, "Of course I can't hack into your cloud server … But I can make it look like I can."

"What?"

"I didn't need to meet with your captain. I just needed you to call him." She nodded toward his hand, holding his cell phone. "I noticed your wireless was secure, but your bluetooth wasn't. My computer just hacked your phone and got your captain's cell number. The police will track him in a few minutes."

Farmboy's lips pulled back in a snarl. He strode to Happy, grabbing his gun, but suddenly stopped at the sound of a shotgun being primed.

"Drop the guns," said a deep voice with a Hispanic accent.

Jane hadn't expected them to have gotten so close to the camp. She turned to see Alex's friends with rifles and shotguns closing in on them. One had snuck up on the driver of the Challenger. With the man's rifle pressed to the back of his head, the driver dropped his gun away from Alex.

Farmboy circled around, his mouth open. "What the—"

"There's exactly twelve of us," said a tall man with a cowboy hat who had appeared from behind the mobile trailer. "Counting you five and the two guards you stationed on that ridge behind us, we've got you outnumbered."

Within seconds, all of them were disarmed and Alex's friends began tying them up with the zip ties they'd brought with them. Farmboy started cussing in Filipino as he was tied.

Jane's hands began to shake, and she clenched them together.

It was over.

"Are you all right?" Alex was in front of her, his hand not quite touching her face.

Her cheek felt hot, and it throbbed. "What were you thinking?"

"What do you mean? It went off without a hitch. Sort of." He winced.

"You weren't supposed to get caught." Her legs were starting to shake, too. She sank down onto a chair by the folding table.

His hands closed over her shoulders. His look was serious. "I wasn't about to let you walk in here by yourself."

"I was afraid for you."

He touched the puffiness at the side of her face. "If I hadn't been here, they might have hurt you even worse."

"But I knew your friends were here."

The truth hit her with a thud of her heartbeat. She'd been nervous. She'd been afraid for Alex. And she certainly hadn't liked being knocked around. But she hadn't felt alone. Because the entire time, she'd never been alone.

She knew there was something there that she would need to think about later.

"Detective Carter's on his way," said a voice in Spanish.

Jane saw Jorge clambering over brush and rocks from behind where the Challenger was parked on the pitted road.

"Jorge, you were supposed to stay in your lunch wagon," Alex said to him in Spanish. "Adelita's going to kill us."

"So is Detective Carter. I think he didn't like us cowboys doing his job."

"His job?" The man with the cowboy hat, a rancher named Emory Valdez, had an innocent expression. "We saw our good friend Alex being kidnapped by these guys and followed him to rescue him. Not our fault they drove up to a meth lab."

Meth lab. Funny how she couldn't smell the fumes anymore. Her head felt as big as a basketball. Stars began to crowd the edges of her vision.

She didn't remember hitting the ground.

8

J ane was alone again. She really shouldn't be surprised.

The rest of the day was a blur. She had woken up lying on the ground with Alex yelling at her. So she'd yelled back—or more like whispered back—for him to keep his voice down.

Detective Carter arrived within minutes. Paramedics arrived half an hour later, but by then Jane had moved to sit on a rock far away from the toxic gases of the meth lab and was feeling better. She was relieved when the paramedics dressed Alex's gunshot wound.

At the police station, Alex's mama had yelled and cried and hugged him and scolded him. She also spent a lot of time alternately poking at and then crying over his gunshot wound. His mama had cried and hugged Jane, too, and her embrace had smelled like apricots and pies. Jane hadn't wanted to let her go.

Detective Carter was dating Jane's Aunt Becca, and so all of Jane's cousins came to the station to make sure she was all right. Maybe to make up for the fact that her own parents were absent.

But Alex and his family had gone back to their farmhouse. Jorge and Adelina and Alex's friends—neighboring ranchers, farmhands, and farmers—had gone home after giving their statements. The Grants had gone back to their mansion outside of Sonoma.

Jane entered her empty apartment and began to cry.

She shut the door quickly, but her legs failed her and she slid to the floor. It was just the shock. She was responding to the stress of the past two days.

No. She was crying because Alex had been trying to tell her something, and she'd turned away. God had been trying to tell her something, and she hadn't wanted to hear.

Hadn't God failed her? Hadn't He allowed Derek and then her father to rip gigantic holes in her chest?

Why had He allowed these people to hurt her?

But He hadn't allowed Farmboy to kill her. Their desperate plan had worked. Detective Carter had said they had picked up the Tumibay captain, the Oyster, within an hour of the accountant's phone call to him.

Jane and Alex were safe.

She rubbed her cheek and jaw, still sore from the blow Farmboy had given to her. Safe, but not unscathed.

They had done a good thing today. That was worth a blow to the jaw.

She grudgingly admitted there was good that had come out of her pain from a year ago. She had broken the chains of her father's disapproval. She had discovered Derek's lies and left EMRY.

With all these things that should free her, why did she feel so alone?

She was cried out. She crawled across the floor to the living room couch, shoved some books and cables off the cushions, and climbed into it.

One of the things that dropped to the floor was her Bible.

It lay in a forlorn heap, pages rippling. She immediately picked it up and smoothed the wrinkles.

Her bookmark was still in place. She'd been reading the Bible in a year when everything happened with Derek and her father, and she hadn't opened it since. It was in Jeremiah, a book she hadn't understood very well at all.

The Lord appeared to us in the past, saying:
"I have loved you with an everlasting love;
I have drawn you with loving-kindness.
I will build you up again
and you will be rebuilt, O Virgin Israel.
Again you will take up your tambourines
and go out to dance with the joyful."

She couldn't stop reading these two verses as she lay curled up on the couch. She was loved. Derek's betrayal and her father's rejection had devastated her because it made her feel so unloveable. But she was loved with a love she was starting to realize she couldn't comprehend.

And that love could heal her. Rebuild her life.

She crushed the Bible to her chest. It was as if she were hiding in a closet and there was a gentle whisper at the closed door. *I am here for you.*

She hesitated, then said, *Come in.*

EPILOGUE

The Villa farmhouse was loud and warm from the people crowded into it. Jane would normally have felt claustrophobic, but she was happy.

One reason was because she'd finally tasted Alex's mama's cooking, and she wanted to move in so she could have that amazing food every single day. At the moment, everyone was waiting for the apricot *empanada* pies to come out of the oven, and the buttery scent of their crusts was filling the house.

Another reason was because she had a chance to thank each of Alex's friends, his own personal cavalry, who had helped last week to take down Farmboy and his associates. Some of them had known Alex in prison. Some were friends of the Villa family. They all had been glad for the chance to help stop the Tumibays.

And a third reason was because she'd had her last day at work today. As of tomorrow, she was making a go of her own business, and the party tonight was an appropriate send-off.

Throughout the evening, she hadn't had much time to speak to Alex, but now he pulled her away from staring at the oven. "The *empanadas* will come out soon. I want to show you something." He grabbed a quilt from the couch before leading her out the back door.

The motion-sensing floodlights turned on as soon as they stepped off the back porch into the yard. Fruit trees lined the yard on three sides, and half the yard was taken up by his mama's vegetable garden, where the shapes of kale and leeks were gilded by the light.

He led her to a trellised bench set in the far corner. Grape vines had been trained into the lattice, and they were just starting to mist with green from new leaves.

They sat, and he draped the quilt over them both. "Edward built this for Mama. I trained the grape vines."

"Do you get grapes?"

"Yes, but they're sour." He made a face, and she laughed. "I have great news. Detective Carter said that they managed to unmount that second hidden partition on the laptop, and it had all the information on how the accountant was going to set me up. I am officially cleared of suspicion."

She squeezed him tight. "I know that was bothering you."

"They also found the name of a police officer who was on the Tumibays' payroll."

Her mouth dropped open. "I know we speculated about the gang having someone at the station who would search traffic cam footage for my car, but it seems so much more awful to find out it was true."

"Detective Carter also said that customs official we found led the FBI to the Tumibays' ephedrine supplier in the Philippines. The gang won't be getting any more of it shipped to the Port of San Francisco."

"That'll stop the meth production?"

"I'd like to think so, but ..." He grimaced. "At the very least, it'll slow things down for them while they search for a new supplier."

"Hopefully Detective Carter will get a bit of break."

"He might try to talk to you later."

"About what?"

"I mentioned how you could have found that second hidden

partition in the hard drive so much faster, and that now that you're starting your own contracting business, maybe the Sonoma PD could hire you once in a while."

"I'll take any work I can get. Uncle Aggie has hired me to write new software to integrate the reservations for both the Joy Luck Life Spa and the hotel."

"How was your last day at work today?"

"I said goodbye to everyone, which was sad, but turning in my security badge was … great." She smiled. "I'm glad they let me give only a week's notice rather than two."

"Are you going to like writing software all the time?"

"It's what I'm best at."

He leaned closer to her. "But is it what you enjoy doing?"

"It used to be. That's why I think it can be, again."

The floodlights switched off, and he said, "Look up."

The clear night sky unfolded over them. It wasn't black, but a deep, deep blue, and the stars looked like they were hanging just over the top of the trellis. She felt his chest expand as he breathed in the night air.

"It reminds me that God is bigger than any of my problems," he said.

"It makes me feel loved," Jane said.

His arm tightened around her.

"I wrote software for EMRY up until a year ago."

"You don't have to tell me," he said.

"Do you want to know?"

He hesitated only a second. "Yes," he whispered.

"My boss was Derek Wallace, and I thought I loved him."

"Is he the one you were dating when we first met?"

"I told you I was interested in him, but we weren't dating. But he gave every indication that he was interested in me. EMRY was a startup, and we worked sixty hours a week together. We wrote a powerful voice recognition software program. Whenever I wrote a piece of code that was especially brilliant, he was affectionate and appreciative. And I kept wanting to please him. You probably know why."

In answer, his hand rubbed her arm.

"We were having a problem with the program, and I had lunch with an old college girlfriend working for a company who makes bluetooth headsets. After I explained what I was working on, she told me about a software engineer at her company who's been working on vocal optimization for their headsets, and how this engineer has found a way to adjust for slurring and incidental throat and lip noise. I told Derek I'd talk to the engineer to ask for any ideas he could give me that wouldn't violate his non-disclosure agreement with his company, but Derek ..." She swallowed. This was still difficult to talk about. "Derek wanted me to offer the engineer money to steal his software from his company and give it to EMRY."

Alex's expression was shocked. "He actually asked you to do that?"

"I refused. Derek was livid. I had thought he ... cared for me, but he said that he only pretended to like me because I was 'smarter' when he paid attention to me."

Alex's muscles had turned rigid. "So he just strung you along like that?"

"It doesn't hurt anymore. That's why I can tell you this. I think it actually hasn't hurt in a long time, but I was in pain for other reasons, and so I didn't notice."

"At least he didn't get the software, did he?"

"Derek went to the engineer himself and got it from him. He used the code to finish EMRY's voice recognition program."

"That's why you left EMRY?"

"I knew it was only a matter of time before Derek fired me, but he wanted to keep using me for my software skills as long as I stayed. Dad didn't want me to quit. That's why we argued. I couldn't stay, because that would be like pretending Derek's behavior was okay. Dad told me essentially to just suck it up. That I was exaggerating. That EMRY was going IPO soon and I'd be stupid to throw away all that money. Dad and I had a huge shouting match, and I walked out and quit EMRY the next day. A few months later, EMRY was bought by Google and my father was livid that I'd been so stupid."

"You weren't stupid," he said.

"I know, but at the time, I doubted myself. Derek wasn't done— I had signed an NDA, so he knew I couldn't say anything about what he'd told me to do, but maybe he was afraid I'd find a way around that. He spread rumors about me to other companies I might have worked for, and the only job I could find was working IT at half what I had been making. I felt so betrayed by everyone, including God. I thought God should have protected me for doing the right thing." Jane took a deep breath, and smelled rosemary and basil. "But it was right for me to leave EMRY, and if I'd gone to another software company, I would still be working for them rather than starting my own business."

She turned her head, rested her brow in the curve of his neck. His skin was warm. "Derek hadn't really loved me, and my father had showed how little he regarded me. This past year, I felt unloveable. And very alone."

"Derek is scum. And your father shouldn't have made you feel that way."

"I'm starting to realize that maybe he did. Because otherwise, I'd still be striving after his approval rather than discovering what God's love really is. I didn't understand God's love, because I'd thought it was like my father's love. But the way God loves me is different. It's real, and it's nonjudgmental, and it's unfailing."

There was a heartbeat of silence, then he whispered, "I love you, too."

She smiled.

He dipped his head and kissed her. His lips were cold, but his kiss was fervent. His hand tilted her face up, then caressed her cheek, her jaw, her neck. He kissed her as if there was nothing else in the world he wanted more, and yet there was also a tenderness as if she was more precious to him than breath.

He pulled back, but his face was still close enough that she could feel the warmth coming off his skin.

"I've never been kissed before," she said.

His smile was bright white, his dimples dark against his tanned cheeks. He kissed her again.

Much, much later, she said, "I want you to come car shopping with me tomorrow."

He gave her a curious look. "Okay … Why the sudden urge?"

"It was Dad who convinced me to get the hybrid."

Alex grinned at her. "What car did you really want?"

"What I'm going to get tomorrow. A Mustang. Cherry red."

He leaned in for another kiss. "Why am I not surprised?"

CONNECT WITH CAMY

Dear friends,

Thanks for joining me on another adventure in Sonoma, California! I love this small town with a big heart, which is also a popular destination for tourists.

Those of you who have read my Sonoma series will recognize Jane and Alex, who were minor characters in *Formula for Danger*. They were both so fascinating to me, with Jane's scarring and relationship with the Grant sisters, and Alex's painful past. They also seemed to have a bit of chemistry in *Formula For Danger* which I couldn't explore since that was Rachel and Edward's story, so I knew I had to give Jane and Alex their own story.

If you'd like to know each time I have a new release or a sale on one of my books, sign up for my newsletter. After a few welcome emails, I only send one or two emails a month.

Camy

Connect with Camy

Get *The Wedding Kimono* free when you join Camy's Newsletter

Join Camy's Patreon

www.ingramcontent.com/pod-product-compliance
Lightning Source LLC
Chambersburg PA
CBHW031209260626
47169CB00004B/1305